·

E D S O N

EDSON

by Bill Morrissey

Alfred A. Knopf   New York   1996

THIS IS A BORZOI BOOK
PUBLISHED BY ALFRED A. KNOPF, INC.

Library of Congress Cataloging-in-Publication Data

Morrissey, Bill.

Edson / by Bill Morrissey. — 1st ed.

p.   cm.

ISBN 0-679-44629-X

1. City and town life—New England—Fiction.   2. Men—New England—
Psychology—Fiction.   3. Working class—New England—Fiction.
4. Musicians—New England—Fiction.   I. Title.

PS3563.087493E37   1996

813'.54—dc20   95-49358

CIP

Manufactured in the United States of America
First Edition

To Ellen

EDSON

THE FIRST SNOWSTORM of the year snuck into New Hampshire as a light dusting that blew itself off the road as soon as it touched down, as if apologizing for the inconvenience. But no one was fooled. People hurried about their business, eyeing the clouds as they loaded the last of the cordwood into garages and cellars, finished weather-stripping the windows, inspected snow blowers and told themselves they might be able to coax one more season out of them. At dusk the wind died down and the wisps of snow gave way to fat white flakes. The leaves still on the hardwood trees and the needles on the evergreens trapped the snow until the weight forced the branches to point to the ground. The season had suddenly changed.

Henry Corvine followed the tire grooves in the snow on the looping two-lane that led into Edson, alternately gassing and letting up on the accelerator to keep his fifteen-year-old Chevy from fishtailing. When he came to a straightaway he took his hands off the wheel to see if the car would stay in the grooves by itself, but it wouldn't. He eased up on the gas as he took hold of the wheel again and guided the big sedan back on track. At the town line his headlights flashed on a statue of the Blessed Virgin set up on a knoll between the road and the Edson River. Keeping her back to the town, she greeted each oncoming car with her palms open at her sides, her shoulders hiked in a permanent shrug as if to say, "Welcome to Edson. It's not my fault."

Henry crossed the bridge where the river switched back under the road and the two-lane became Main Street. He was surprised to find it still unplowed. Edson's road crew took great pride in its reputation as the best snow removal team on New Hampshire's seacoast. Henry pictured the huge yellow plows covered with snow, sitting dumbfounded in the town lot like the ships at Pearl Harbor. He downshifted to second as the road sloped and curved, becoming a slick carpet of packed snow between the buildings that defined downtown Edson. The Tanner Shoe Company, an asymmetrical stretch of reddish-gray buildings so old and grimy they seemed to repel the snow, lined the length of the river side of Main Street, its hundreds of tiny black windows looking across the road at the shops, stores, luncheonettes, and small businesses on the other side. Henry coasted to a stop in front of Martello's Fruit and Real Estate, the only store open on Sunday night. He needed cigarettes, beer, and milk, and maybe a few other things he'd remember once he was inside. The red, green, and white lights from Martello's sign, mixed with the falling snow, gave an eerie Christmas glow to the downtown. It was only the first week of November. Henry left the Chevy idling at the curb.

Martello's was deep and narrow, shaped like a boxcar, and crammed with canned goods, hip waders, baked goods, magazines, panty hose, videos, cigarettes, shot shells, fresh fruit, flannel shirts, packaged deli meats, snacks, aspirin, and beer. The beer cooler took up the entire rear wall and a third of one of the side walls. Henry stomped the snow off his hunting boots and walked across the newspapers spread over the oily floor to the beer cooler. He liked the way Martello's smelled; it reminded him of summer camp. He picked out a six-pack of Miller pints, moved to the dairy bin for a quart of milk and a bar of Monterey Jack cheese, then added a loaf of bread, a package of baloney, and a fishnet bag of oranges. He checked the expiration date on the milk. He carried everything to the counter and said, "A couple of cigarettes, please, Deb."

Debbie, at sixteen the youngest of the Martello girls, was propping herself up with her forearms splayed across a section of the Boston Sunday *Globe*. Her chin dug sharply into her collarbone as she strained to read something at the bottom of the page without shifting her position. At Henry's request she reached up to the rack above her head and, with the unconscious knowledge of repetition, took down a pack of Merits and a pack of Kool Milds. She dropped the cigarettes next to the six-pack, then straightened up and, for the first time, looked at him. Her eyes, the color of sky-blue wallpaper hung too long in a sunny room, flicked around his face from ear to ear several times before finally settling on the top of the magazine rack behind him. "Is that it?" she asked.

"That's it."

"You want a bag?"

"Please." Henry reached for the Merits, opened the pack, and lit one, his first cigarette in five days. He sucked the warm smoke far into his lungs and exhaled slowly, savoring the taste. As he reached for his wallet, he felt the room begin to spin pleasantly. His hands felt like they were filled with helium.

"You get your deer yet?" she asked.

He shook his head. "Only two partridge."

She rang up the sale and bagged his groceries. Henry tapped his finger on the newspaper and asked what she was reading.

"Oh, this thing on Mary Lou Retton and the Olympics," she said. "I wonder what the hell she's doing these days. Haven't heard anything about her in a long time. Look at this picture, will you? Jesus Christ, her mouth is bigger than her head."

Henry agreed, then asked if they'd been busy all day with the snow.

"Jesus Christ, up to half an hour ago it was a regular stampede in here. Christ, I ain't even finished the sports section yet." Then she wiped her mouth and shifted her weight back to her forearms. Her head drooped as she scanned the paper for something else to read.

Henry dragged on his cigarette as he left the store,

stopping on the granite steps outside to adjust the bag with a quick punch of his hip. Then he saw the yellow spinning lights of the snowplows at the southern end of Main. He listened to the low booms and clunks and back-up bells as the blades were lowered, then the scraping of metal against the macadam in the town offices' parking lot, always the first part of Edson to be plowed. The reflection of the swirling lights in the black mill windows gave Henry the impression that that part of the mill had been converted into a nightclub. He shook his head and laughed to himself, picturing a disco with a textile theme, or maybe a union theme. "Dinner for six in the Emma Goldman Room? Well, yes, I believe there *is* dancing tonight, sir." He coughed on his last drag, then flipped the cigarette into the snow. Light-headed from the smoke, he climbed back into the Chevy and drove home.

Prescott Arms, the residence hotel where Henry rented a studio apartment, had originally been the home of Isaac Tanner, the founder of the mill. Set high on the southeastern face of a hill, it looked down over homes, shops, and businesses to the front of the mill. In 1913 a fire destroyed a third of the house and badly damaged the rest. Tanner, by then retired, responded by building three houses, each larger than the original, on nine acres along newly cleared Elm Street. He moved himself into the middle and largest, then moved his two sons, who ran the mill, into the adjacent houses. Eventually the original house was sold to a developer and repaired enough to open as a residential hotel, but even from the beginning it always seemed in need of paint or shingles or lawn mowing or paying tenants, and in its gradual, determined decline it now housed pensioners, students, the young and transient, the insane, the unemployed or unemployable, the newly separated or divorced.

Henry parked in his usual spot. The back lot hadn't been plowed, which meant he'd have to dig himself out the next morning after the plows came and buried him in. He turned the Chevy off and waited while it shuddered and hacked up a cloud of smoke. Stepping out, he set the bag from Martello's on the roof and opened the rear door. From the backseat he took his .50 Hawken rifle, a new twenty-gauge over-and-under shotgun, and partridge. He slipped the straps of his possibles kit and clothes bag over his shoulder and carried everything up the slippery back stairs.

He had taken the partridge that morning before the snow, when the low-pressure front caused them to hole up in a stand of white pine. It had been his first double ever on partridge, two going-away shots, both left to right. Each bird crumpled immediately, one folding and dropping into the brittle mesh of a blowdown, the other into a dead juniper.

At the third-floor landing he pulled the door open and walked down the dimly lit hall on a spongy carpet that made little wet breathing sounds with each step. His apartment was at the end, beyond two other apartments halfway down the hall. Rachel Creelman and Caroline Laine, both in their early twenties, shared the apartment on the right. Larry Davenport lived across from them. He was older—Henry's age, thirty-seven—and worked in the shipping department at the mill. Henry had lived at the hotel five weeks before noticing the business card tacked to the frame above Larry's door. On the back of it Larry had written: *Desolation Row*.

Henry's apartment was colder and darker than the hallway, lit only by the edge of floodlight from the parking lot. He bit the string to the fluorescent overhead light and yanked it with his head. As it blinked on and off and on, he dropped everything on the bed, then went to the nightstand to turn the table lamp on. He quickly pulled off the overhead. That light belonged in a doctor's office, he thought, or some Motor Vehicle Department clerk's. Henry switched the space heater to high, picked up the two birds strung together with a shoelace, and put them in the refrigerator. He sat down, considering how many things there were to do. Pulling a beer from the bag, he opened it and took a long drink, then lit a Kool Mild and slapped a cassette of Johnny Hodges into the boom box on the nightstand. He unlaced and kicked off his hunting boots, then his stiff brier-proofs. Mail, he remembered. He slipped into sweatpants and walked down the hall to Rachel and Caroline's.

Rachel opened the door when he knocked. Leaning against the jamb, she crossed her arms. She wore a long-tailed corduroy shirt, moccasins, and thick red wool socks. "Hi," she said.

"All dressed up for your date already?" he said, looking down at her bare legs.

She fixed her gaze on Henry in a way that dared him to look anywhere but into her eyes. She reached behind her back, lifted the shirttails and adjusted her panties, then let the shirttails drop. She folded her arms again. "So how's the great white hunter?"

"Two partridge."

She made a sour face.

"You ever had partridge, Rachel?"

"Never had canary either," she said.

Caroline came to the door, holding a plate and a dish towel. "Hi, Henry," she said. "You get your deer?"

"Gross," Rachel said.

Henry ignored Rachel. "No, not yet. Two birds but no Bambi." He smelled spaghetti coming from their kitchen.

"I heard Romeo Oulette shot a six-point buck that went a hundred and thirty pounds dressed."

"My birds are about that size," Henry said.

Caroline smiled and ran the dish towel over the dry plate, while Rachel disappeared inside.

"Was there any mail?" Henry asked.

"Just some bills," she said.

"Oh."

"Were you expecting something?"

Henry caught himself staring at her breasts, but could just as well have been staring at anything. Now that he was home, his energy was slipping away and he couldn't stop it or even want to. He blinked and looked off to the side.

"Henry?"

"I was—some photos from Texas—but it's not important."

"I'll get your mail," she said. "Come on in if you want."

Henry stood in the doorway as Caroline scooped up his mail from an island counter in the kitchen. "Thanks," he said. "That old guy down at the desk leaves the mail lying around everywhere."

"Oh, I know. He's awful. Are you going up to the Millhouse tonight?"

"Maybe later. I think I need a shower and a nap first."

"You do look beat," she said.

"I am. Anyway, thanks again." Then he remembered he'd left his cigarette burning and rushed back to his apartment, to find the stub angled down, safely smoldering in the ashtray. He ground it out and lit another, then sat down on the bed and took off his sweatpants. The cigarettes still made him dizzy after the five-day layoff at the hunting cabin. He took a long drink of beer, then checked a pocket in his travel bag and found six more Nicorettes. He was smoking again, anyway. The warmth from the space heater hit him quickly and, combined with the beer and the cigarette, gently eased him into slow motion. Ben Webster joined Johnny Hodges on a Duke Ellington tune. When he was tired, Henry preferred instrumental music. To follow a story line seemed like too much of an effort when all he wanted was to feel the rhythms and textures as his mind wandered away from any immediate concerns. While he listened, Henry took off the rest of his clothes and wrapped himself in his bathrobe. He poured two fingers of bourbon into a mug.

When the phone rang, he turned down the volume on

the answering machine and drank his bourbon. He sat on the bed and turned the music up a little. Finishing his cigarette, he set his alarm for nine, took a long shower, and went to bed.

RACHEL SAT at the kitchen counter while Caroline finished the dishes.

The kitchen was a tiny corner blocked off from the rest of the apartment by a narrow island long enough for two stools. Set against the wall was a small table and three chairs. The cupboard was painted white with flat yellow trim. The gas stove and the refrigerator were white, though the side of the fridge facing the stove was graying and flecked with rust. On the table, Caroline kept a small vase with six dried flowers. Their bedrooms were at opposite ends of the apartment, Caroline's off the kitchen and Rachel's off the living room.

Caroline wiped a saucepan dry and set it back in the cupboard. "What were you doing out there without any pants on?"

"It was only Henry," Rachel said. "I was, like, changing when he knocked."

"But you didn't know it was Henry. Besides, he's asked you out a couple times, and that was like teasing him. Nobody likes being teased."

Rachel spun around slowly on her stool, then reversed

direction. "Yeah, like Henry really thinks I'm teasing him. What time is it?" She jumped from the stool and walked to the CD player across the room. "Roger will be here soon enough. I'd better get ready." She ran her finger down a stack of discs piled on a speaker.

"Where are you going tonight?" Caroline asked.

"We were going to a movie in Newington, but I don't think the roads are going to be in any shape to travel. It's, like, still coming down."

"So what're you going to do?"

Rachel opened her mouth and ran her tongue around her lips, knowing it would embarrass Caroline, then said, "We'll more than likely end up at the Millhouse."

"That's where I'm going."

"What a surprise. Where else can you go on a night like this?"

"The Polish Club," Caroline said.

Rachel gave her an incredulous look, then walked to the window. Lifting the shade, she smeared a warm hand across the glass and squinted through the window, which had gone nubbly with ice. "Yeah, Edson's answer to the question nobody ever asked: the Polish Club." She slowly drew out the name. She had a way of repeating something Caroline said to make it sound idiotic, but Caroline rarely detected any nastiness in Rachel's tone and didn't get angry or feel hurt.

Rachel let the shade drop. "This snow sucks. It really sucks!"

Caroline thought about the Polish Club as she hung up the dish towel. Besides the Eagles and the Legion, there were the Riverside Inn, more of a restaurant with a tiny lounge, and the Millhouse, the only bar with live music. But the Millhouse was mostly patronized by students from the university in Durham, ex-students, musicians, people without jobs, music fans who came from as far away as Boston to hear certain performers. At the Millhouse you didn't see the same people you saw in the bars downtown. It didn't really belong in Edson. Like an exchange student who never went back home.

The Polish Club, though, was the cleanest bar in town. There were never any fights, and the beer was the cheapest. It had been there since the big immigration of 1913, when there was a shortage of Yankee and French-Canadian laborers. The Catholic Church and Isaac Tanner sent a representative to Poland, and he brought back the entire population of Czwykla. With the financial help of the Church, the mill provided new housing and employment, allowing the Poles to slip through U.S. Immigration easily. Edson became one-third French, one-third Yankee, and nearly one-third Polish. Our Lady of the Immaculate Conception flourished that year with all its new parishioners, and ground was broken for the American Club of Polish Descent—membership open to all, officeholders required to be at least half Polish. Caroline always enjoyed herself at the club, and it was where most of her old high school classmates would be that night. She wondered why Rachel reacted the way she did, then wondered if Rachel knew something about the club that she didn't.

At twenty-one, she found bars and drinking new and sometimes puzzling. The one afternoon she and Suzie Martello, her best friend, went to the Legion, it took her eyes what seemed like a full minute to adjust to the darkness, and she could see the old men sitting like question marks on their stools around the bar, watching the baseball game silently, almost grimly, sipping their beers and whiskey as if this were their job and they were having a bad day.

In Portsmouth she saw the other extreme—well-lit bars with live music and patios and decks overlooking the river, people drinking white wine or piña coladas or Canadian beer and acting like they were on vacation. The Pilot Inn, where she and Rachel worked, was like that. This was the first waitressing job she'd ever looked forward to. Even in the winter, when the deck was closed and covered with snow, the low sunlight reflecting off the water would pour through the restaurant. She loved the way it jittered on the walls. She had worked there almost two years now, and that was where she'd met Rachel. On slow, snowy days she sometimes would just stand with a coffee in front of the glass doors to the deck, watching the tugs and freighters, or the chimney smoke rising up from the houses across the river in Maine.

On Sunday nights the Millhouse held an open mike, and most of the local acoustic musicians showed up to do a set, jam, socialize, and drink, though the performers never got paid in actual dollars and cents. Instead, they received a free roast-beef dinner and all the beer they could drink. Caroline had never listened to folk music before, but she liked it right from the beginning and by now knew many of the performers and had her favorites.

Rachel cursed the snow again and walked back to the stack of CDs on the speaker. "Let's see," she muttered.

"It's on the bookshelf," Caroline said.

"What is?"

"Tyler Beckett. That's what you're looking for, isn't it?"

Rachel pursed her lips as if to say, So what? She turned to the bookshelf, where other CDs were stacked, and ran her hands through her hair, lifting it up above her head like a handful of wheat-colored yarn and letting it fall back over her shoulders. When she found the Tyler Beckett CD she held it up like a hand mirror, then opened the jewel box and slipped the disc into the player.

"What time's Roger picking you up?" Caroline asked.

"Seven, seven-thirty."

"Well, do you want to shower first, then?"

"No, you go ahead," Rachel said, turning up the volume. "He's always late. Anyway, I want to hear the first couple songs." She flopped down on the divan and curled up around a large pillow.

Caroline walked back to her room and closed the door.

Tyler Beckett was a songwriter from New York City who sang her sophisticated, somewhat detached lyrics in a soft, equally detached voice. Her debut album—catching the public, the music industry, and the media by surprise —had squeezed into the top ten on the national pop charts earlier in the year on the strength of a catchy but un-danceable single called "Avenue C." She was more often compared to Grace Paley than to Joni Mitchell. The sound was unique, the look was right, and the timing was perfect.

In a matter of weeks, Tyler Beckett's trademark white beret, white scarf, and horn-rimmed glasses became as common a sight on the New Hampshire campuses as flannel shirts. Rachel played the album constantly. Though Caroline liked her well enough, she didn't enjoy hearing young women from the college sing Tyler Beckett songs over and over again at the Millhouse on Sunday nights.

Rachel turned up the CD player. Caroline heard it clearly in her room as she undressed in front of her mirror. Rachel always played the stereo too loud, she thought, dropping her clothes in the hamper and pulling on her bathrobe. She laid out her clothes for the night on the bed, then walked to the bathroom. Halfway there, she saw the crack of yellow light beneath the door. She glanced at the divan—Rachel was gone—and could hear the shower running when she turned off the CD player. "Jerk," she said in the empty room, then marched back to her bedroom. From the drawer in her night table she took a pack of Marlboro Lights, a book of matches, and an ashtray. She covered the crack beneath her door with a towel. It wasn't so much that Rachel had jumped into the shower before her; it was that she'd done it without telling her, as if she weren't even there.

Caroline opened the window ten inches and the storm window a little less, then felt the black cold air rush in. She sat down and switched on a six-inch fan that faced the window. Tightening her bathrobe against the cold, she lit the cigarette and blew each drag outside. When she finished, she dropped the butt out the window, wiped the ashtray with a Kleenex, and dropped that out too, so no scent of smoke would remain. Then she put everything back in the drawer and sprayed the room with air freshener. She took a taste of mouthwash and swallowed. Rachel forbade smoking in the apartment and didn't even know Caroline had started.

She walked back into the living room, heard the whine of Rachel's hair dryer, and returned to her room. Sitting at the vanity, she took off her barrette and let her hair fall forward. It was the darkest of browns, almost black, and as straight as pencil leads. She had been growing her hair out for six months, and now it covered the top of her shoulders. She gathered and pulled it back tightly behind her head. Though full, it always felt too fine to her. She wished she had Rachel's long, thick hair, which always looked great even though Rachel never seemed to do anything with it. Caroline let her hair fall back down and began brushing it while she waited for the shower.

HIS ALARM tripped at nine o'clock, a sudden malicious buzz jerking him somewhere back into the world. Henry propped himself up on one elbow in the dark room, his free arm flapping around the nightstand for the clock. It couldn't possibly be time to get up, he thought. He'd just shut his eyes.

His hand found the snooze alarm, and he pushed it in with his thumb. Neither awake nor asleep, he could've been anywhere, at any time. All he knew was that he was beyond exhaustion and wanted simply to fall back asleep in the darkness until something absolutely forced him to take some sort of action.

Then, for a moment, his heart stuttered with panic as he thought he was back in Alaska, where he had spent the past summer as a deckhand on a purse seiner. He hadn't fished commercially for salmon in ten years but had gone out just five months ago, in June, for one last season, to make some cash, and on opening day had abruptly aged from twenty-seven to thirty-seven. Once they began to haul back the first set, Henry discovered he was no longer strong enough to do the job. His arms and legs trembled as he rushed in to gather armfuls of web pouring down from the power block high above the deck. He dragged the heavy, soaked web back to the edge, fanning it out like a bridal train so the next set would roll out smoothly. He repeated this over and over, stacking the web higher, stumbling over the top of it as he charged in again, gasping for air. His fingers twitched uncontrollably. His legs burned. Jellyfish rained down on him from the descending web and clung to the rim of his sweatshirt hood like long red strands of mucus. When he snapped his neck to flip the jellyfish away, the globs whipped into his eyes and blinded him until tears washed them clean a minute or two later, but the pace of the work never let up just because he couldn't see. He thought of the twenty-hour workday ahead and of the three days left to the first opening of the season and knew he had committed himself to a job he could no longer perform. But there was no way to quit.

He was on a work boat, and land was a vague silhouette through the morning fog.

After the first set, the four crewmen—soaked and breathless, but out of the rain—gathered around the galley table and sucked down steaming coffee. John, the cook, the fifth man on the boat, took a cup for himself and one for the skipper, up on the flying bridge. Henry's hands fluttered as he lit a cigarette.

"You okay, Henry?" McManus, the corkline man, asked. "You don't look so good."

He and McManus had fished together for the same skipper years before and had become friends. Five years younger than Henry, McManus hadn't fished in years either, but he was in better shape and seemed to be having an easier time of it.

"I'll be okay," Henry said. "I just gotta get back into it." But his body was already spent, empty, and he had to summon up something from deep inside so as not to humiliate himself in front of an old friend. There were another nineteen sets that day.

Somehow he made it, but that night McManus had to help him up into his top bunk, both of them punchy from the work and the rain and the cold. At dinner, they met the good-natured gibes of the rest of the crew with silence. Afterward Henry poured a tall drink of straight Irish whiskey from a bottle he kept in his bunk to share with McManus, who slept across from him on the port side in the peak of the forecastle. Henry had learned in his first year that a large, quick shot of whiskey after a day's work counteracted the adrenaline surging through him, allowing him to take full advantage of the three and a half hours of sleep before the next day's fishing started.

After the drink Henry stripped off his wet clothes, lay down, and had just shut his eyes when the engine suddenly began grinding and the forecastle door slammed open.

"Let's go! Let's go! Let's go!" Dave Lavernette, the skipper, screamed down into the greasy darkness. "Let's go, Corvine! Get the anchor chain now!" His voice had the urgency and anger of a drill instructor given one last chance.

Because his bunk was directly below the hatch, Henry had been assigned the task of guiding the anchor chain in every morning. The job could just as easily have been given to McManus, but Henry happened to be standing by when the skipper handed out that detail.

He pulled the two-inch string to the bare lightbulb above his bunk at the same time McManus pulled his. They stared at each other in disbelief, two old veterans, as the lights from the other bunks clicked on. Henry shook his head. His muscles had had just enough time to stiffen to a near-paralytic state. He lay in his bunk for a moment, then found the dry pair of dungarees at the foot of his bunk and tried to pull them on. But his fingers were as swollen and boneless as hot dogs, and he couldn't get a grip. His stomach and shoulders felt numb at first; when he tried to move, it was like he broke some kind of seal, and the pain rushed in. Again he wanted more than anything to quit.

That morning it took everything he had, with Mc-Manus pushing his butt, just to pull himself up and out the hatch and guide in the anchor chain. Once they were under way he poured a coffee in the galley, lit a cigarette, and gazed out at the wet, cold, silvery world.

IN EDSON he was warm and dry and could stay in bed as long as he wanted. He switched on the lamp and sat up. Turning the radio to a country station, he lit a cigarette and let fragments of memory wash into his half-sleep. Alaska. The divorce before that. All the miles behind the wheel again. Drunken nights in nameless motels. Phone calls. He leaned his back against the headboard, brought his knees up, and wrapped his arms around them. The space heater blazed a bright hunter's orange. The memories became sharper, and he put them in order—always starting with the May night his wife had come home from work, poured herself a bourbon, and asked him to move out. She'd pulled a stool up to the kitchen counter, where he stood kneading and shaping hamburger patties for supper. He remembered how she apologized and how her hands shook when she took a drink, how the glass clicked against her teeth.

"Is there someone else?" he asked.

"No," she said, and he believed her. She lit a Kool Mild, offered him one, and he accepted. When they met he smoked only Merits, but then he'd started mooching from her and soon enough was hooked on menthols too.

All she ever told him was that she didn't want to be married to him anymore, or to anyone else ever again, and nothing he could do or say could make her change her mind. He expected his eyes to well up with tears and his heart to fill with pain, but instead it was as if he were not a participant in his own breakup but a passive observer. He remembered thinking, though, that nothing would ever make sense again. Two weeks later he phoned his old skipper, signed on again, and left the next week for Beaufort, Washington, where the boat was being readied for the season in Alaska.

Now, in Edson, sitting in bed and smoking his cigarette, Henry tried to picture his ex-wife in this snowstorm at their old house in Laconia. He saw her shoveling the snow off the long side porch and the steps, carving a narrow path out to her red Toyota pickup. The pickup was the only new vehicle he'd ever owned.

He lifted his warm, half-finished beer from the nightstand and took a sip. The more he thought about it, the more he wanted to stay in bed and just drink by himself and listen to music. He pulled the blanket over his legs, too exhausted to do anything else. There were plenty of Sundays he could hear music up at the Millhouse. He absently ran his thumb over the tips of his left-hand fingers, where there once had been calluses from guitar strings.

Then he heard Rachel's bedsprings through the thin wall that separated his apartment from her bedroom. A head thunked against the wall, and Henry heard giggling. He flipped the covers off and sat up on the side of the bed. He shook out a fresh cigarette from the pack of Merits an/

finished the beer. While he listened to Rachel laughing, he found clean clothes and dressed. She knew he could hear her, but tonight he didn't want to listen. He found his leather jacket and walked out the door. Some nights he did listen to her. Once, when he was drunk, he even timed them.

CAROLINE LET Pope Johnson buy her another beer. She'd heard him play her first night at the Millhouse, several months ago, and he was still the songwriter she liked the best.

That first night, Pope sang a song about an aging millworker walking home from his job at the Packard Company up in Ashland. She'd never heard a song about New Hampshire before—people wrote about New York City and Texas and California, places in the South, Paris and Rome—and her face flushed with recognition as she lisned. It was as if he was telling the story of her uncle iel, up in Bristol. He'd been stopped one too many times unken driving, and when the town cop asked to see his license, he ripped it out of his wallet, pulled a Zippo work pants, and torched it right in the front seat of t. Most of Pope Johnson's songs that night were ill towns of New Hampshire, and they reminded he old family stories her father told around le when he was in a good mood.

"Y'all wanna hear anything in particular?" Pope asked Caroline. Though he was a New Hampshire native, his accent sounded southern or midwestern, and Caroline mistakenly assumed he'd traveled a great deal. "I gotta go warm up in a minute."

She was flattered that Pope would ask her opinion of anything having to do with music, or could be interested in her in other ways. "I really liked that new one you did last week."

"Oh, yeah? Ya liked that one?"

"Very much."

He nodded and reached for his beer. His face was long and narrow, and his dark eyes had the shine of a wild animal watching prey. The first hint of crow's-feet around his eyes made him look older than his twenty-six years, which Caroline found attractive. He was the opposite of Henry that way, she thought. Henry still could pass for an undergraduate in Durham, though when he and Pope were together it was clear by the way he carried himself that he was older. Pope finished his beer, excused himself, and left for the back room to tune up.

The rumor around the club was that Pope was negotiating a deal with one of the largest independent record companies in the country. But he never discussed his business with anyone—more out of fear of jinxing a deal, he claimed, than anything else. Nonetheless, the rumor raised his status among the other musicians and the audience, and people began discussing the poignant importance of the same songs they'd talked through only weeks earlier.

The Millhouse was crowded, and the audience good-humored and generous with applause. Cross-country skis filled the foyer, lined up against the walls like saplings. The first snowfall always brought out extra customers to the bars in a tiny, unplanned festival heralding the onset of winter. All that was tired and faded and broken was suddenly hidden, if only temporarily, and the air was sharp and sweet with wood smoke. It had to be enjoyed right then, because it was really only a harbinger of the true winter of gray snow, dead batteries, and cold rooms.

Caroline wanted a cigarette, but in a town the size of Edson everything eventually got back to her parents, and she didn't want them to know she had started. The Millhouse was dark, though, almost as dark as the Legion, and she wondered if she could risk it. Most of the Millhouse patrons were from out of town and didn't care if she smoked or not.

THE STREETS were quiet and still and cool, not cold like after a midwinter storm. A few small flakes drifted down and were visible in the cones of streetlight. Six inches of snow clung to the peaked roofs of the tall mill houses. Henry unbuttoned his coat as he walked to the bar. He walked to most places in Edson, partly because he liked to, partly because the Chevy took so long to warm up enough not to stall at every stop sign. He reached into his shirt pocket for a cigarette, then thought again. Once he'd put some distance between himself and the hotel, he slowed his pace and then stopped in the middle of the road. Yellow kitchen light spilled from the rear of the mill houses, across the narrow cement driveways and up the sides of the houses next door. The houses looked huddled together for protection. Henry pushed his hands into his pockets and listened to the distant electronic bleating of a snowplow in reverse. He heard a second plow closer by, as if it were answering the first. Turning to look back up the street, he saw two cross-country skiers coming down the hill on the thin layer of crushed snow left by the plow. They turned left down a side street, toward one of the softball fields.

He had always liked Edson. Over the years he often referred to it as his hometown, and though it wasn't, it would come as close as any town ever would to fitting that description. This was the third time he'd moved to town, having driven directly back from Beaufort after the salmon season. Newly divorced, he had no plans and couldn't think of anywhere else to go.

He first moved to Edson fifteen years earlier, when he was twenty-two. He'd been living in a small mill town in the foothills of the White Mountains. All the towns north of Laconia are small, and Laconia itself isn't too much either.

He was a musician then, a folksinger. There wasn't much work playing acoustic music anywhere in New England, but he managed to pay the rent scratching up après-ski gigs in Waterville Valley and weekend shows in mill-town bars, setting up and taking down his own little PA system, hauling it back and forth in his car. Most of his weekdays were free, and he used that time to write. He *had* to write, just as he *had* to breathe. The audience in the bars, though, wanted to hear songs they knew, and that made for long nights doing mostly covers, occasionally slipping one of his own songs into the four forty-five-minute sets he played each night. He kept at it, slowly improving, chipping away at the beast, losing all track of time with the guitar in his hands. Whole days were lost, punctuated only by phone calls or knocks on the door.

One night at a gig in North Conway, a musician friend told him about a place down in Edson where, on Sundays, performers got free dinner and beer, and where the audience responded to original material. Henry wanted to believe him more than he actually did, but he drove down the next Sunday and discovered it was all true—and that a community of like-minded musicians made the same trek to the Millhouse, playing what they wanted without regard to the pop charts or the usual requests. Every week, Henry made the two-hour drive down, and the longer drive home. He moved to Edson three months later, and stayed for four years, until his first trip to Alaska.

Now, as he walked to the Millhouse, he passed the houses he'd lived and jammed and partied in. He saw lit rooms with the shades drawn and recalled where he'd written certain songs, where he'd met this waitress or that college girl. Exhaustion pushed his thoughts toward the past, and he drifted along, offering no resistance. He crossed under a streetlight and remembered a beer-fueled talk about some horn arrangement he'd had there with his bass player late one night, both of them chain-smoking and slapping mosquitoes.

The money from Alaska would soon run out, and he had no idea what he'd do then. The season had been abruptly aborted, so he hadn't earned as much as he'd hoped.

Passing a basement apartment where he'd lived for a couple of months, he wondered what had happened to his old roommate.

CAROLINE WAVED Larry over to join her. Though they'd met only when she moved into the hotel, she had known of her neighbor across the hall since she was in grammar school. He'd been the captain and star quarterback for the Warriors the last time Edson High won the state division championship or even made the finals. He had a full scholarship at Columbia, and great things were predicted for him. But halfway through his freshman season he quietly returned and took a job in the shipping department at the mill. All he would say was that he didn't like New York City and that football wasn't fun the way they played it.

He greeted Caroline with a loose, worn smile. He hadn't shaved for days. She pulled out the chair next to hers. "You heard about Louis Martineau?" he asked, sitting down.

"The Public Works guy?"

"Yeah." He ordered a pitcher of beer from a passing

waitress and pulled a pack of cigarettes from his overcoat pocket. "He got real drunk watching the Patriots this afternoon down to the Legion."

"And that's why the snowplows were late?"

"Well, I heard two versions. One is that they all showed up early in the afternoon before the snow and got so tanked and into the games that he didn't know or care it was snowing. It's not like the Legion has any picture windows."

"But what about people coming with snow on their coats? And nobody *told* them?"

"No idea. The second version is that he got wicked drunk and belligerent—same as the first—but when the Patriots went into overtime, he wouldn't let his guys get to the snowplows until it was over. And they had the late game today."

"That's not like him," she said.

"Don't I know it."

"The snowplows, though," Caroline said. "I mean, he *lives* for snowstorms."

"That's just what they're saying at the Legion, so who knows?" He looked at her. "Henry get back yet?"

"Yeah, a little after six."

"He get his deer?"

"No," she said. "Two partridge, though."

"Is he coming up here tonight?"

"He said he'd take a nap and come up later, but he looked pretty tired."

After lighting a cigarette, Larry picked up the pitcher and topped off Caroline's beer. She thought about asking him for a smoke to take out behind the bar, then decided against it.

HENRY CAME in the back door and walked through the kitchen to the dressing room, which was really just a storage space with food shelves, an oil tank, compressed-gas tanks, and some beat-up furniture for the musicians.

"Mr. Henry?" Pope Johnson said from the couch.

"Mr. Pope." They'd called each other *Mister* since Pope was a teenager. Henry couldn't remember how it got started. He draped his coat over the tank of compressed gas that powered the taps out front.

"So nice to see y'all out and about at your age with the snow 'n' all," Pope said. "You know, careful of the hips."

"Yeah, and it's nice to see you in men's clothing for a change." That forced a smile out of Pope. Henry also wanted to tell him that "y'all" is plural.

Pope sat on the soft, flat arm of the couch with his guitar across his lap, sipping a beer and smoking a cigarette. He flicked his ash into an overturned hubcap on the floor and said nothing more. Henry had known Pope since he was fourteen—and he was twenty-five, dating Pope's sister—and had taught him his first guitar chords and picking patterns. He hadn't seen him for ten or twelve years, and had no idea Pope had become a musician, until he dropped by the Millhouse his first week back from Alaska.

Henry walked out to the front room. The bartender, who'd bought out the owner while Henry was en route to Beaufort, filled three mugs of beer and carried them to the far end of the bar. The customers paid and took their beers back to their table; she scooped up the change they'd left and dropped it in her jar. Once she saw Henry, she snatched a glass, dropped in a few cubes, and filled it to the brim with Jack Daniel's. As she handed it to him, she pulled a strand of gray hair out in front of her. "Henry, do you think I should start coloring this?"

"No way, Heidi. It looks great. It means you're not a kid."

"Is that good?"

"*I* think so."

"I don't know," she said, tucking the strand away. "I wouldn't mind being a kid again. I sure had a lot more energy when I just waitressed here. I remember listening to you every Sunday. Those were fun times, weren't they? I'd save my break until you got on."

"Well, now you've got Pope Johnson."

"Be nice." She turned his left hand over on the bar and squeezed each fingertip, looking for calluses. "You're still not playing?"

"No." He pulled his hand away and put it in his pocket.

"You really should. It's a different scene now, a lot better than it used to be. More places to play. You could just step in again and take it all over. Put out another record and——"

"I don't think so."

"I've got to get back to work," she said. "I'll talk to you later. Oh, hey! How did those Nicorettes work out?" She had given him several packets to get him through the five-day hunt.

"They worked great, but I'm smoking again now that I'm back in town."

"Well, keep trying."

"Yeah, I know. I'll quit soon enough." Henry had left his menthols in his coat pocket. He returned to the dressing room. Pope was still on the couch with his guitar. Paul Dufresne, a fiddle player from Lowell, sat in a folding chair at the other end of the couch, holding a beer with both hands. He barely looked old enough to drink. He took a deep breath, then forced down two inches of beer. He had only recently started playing the Sunday hoots. Henry tuned out the trio he heard rehearsing a bluegrass standard in the kitchen.

"Nervous?" Pope asked the fiddler, with absolutely no concern in his voice.

"A little bit."

Pope looked over to Henry. "Y'all get your deer this week?" He spoke to Henry in the same flat tone.

"Two partridge, no deer."

"Better than nothing, I reckon."

"You *reckon*, huh? What part of Oklahoma are you from, Pope?"

Pope pretended Henry hadn't said anything. "To tell you the truth, Mr. Henry, I've decided to move to New York City."

"That's a hell of a place." Henry reached into his coat pocket for the cigarettes.

Pope shrugged and reached for his beer on the floor. "*You* of all people should know that's where the business is."

"I thought you were getting a lot of gigs."

"I'm still pumping gas, ain't I? Hey, you want a job, I can get you *my* job."

The dressing room door swung open, and two young women wearing guitars and white scarves hurried in, beaming from the applause. Pope immediately began picking out the chords to Tyler Beckett's hit single, "Avenue C."

Henry thought it was kind of funny, but looked away and lit a cigarette. He wanted to get out of the dressing room.

"Man, it's packed out there tonight," Pope said to him, then turned to Dufresne. "They sound a little frisky out there tonight, don't you think? Y'all got some hot tunes ready for them?"

"I don't know." He took a deep breath to calm himself and drank his beer.

"You're on next, aren't you?" Pope's talk became faster and more staccato.

"After the next act."

"Then I go on," Pope said. "You're just doing solo fiddle, right? That's *all* you're doing, right?"

"Th-that's all I do."

"Hope ya got a lot of fast ones. This is kind of a fast-song crowd, don't ya think?"

Henry went out to listen to the music. He'd seen that kind of psych job done before, and done better. He thought Pope was being a bully simply because he could be. The

Dufresne kid was nervous enough, and certainly no threat. He was so new at performing he couldn't even see what Pope was doing to him. Henry felt better outside the dressing room. He'd had his fill of scenes like that years before.

CAROLINE SAW Henry getting his drink freshened at the bar and turned to Larry. "Has Henry ever paid for a drink in here?"

"Not in years."

"I guess he practically used to live here, right?"

"He owned this town a few years ago," Larry said, standing up and catching Henry's eye. "Or at least this bar."

"He used to own the *bar?*"

"Not literally."

"Caroline!" Suzie Martello pulled out a chair and sat down. She had a blue watch cap pulled down to her eyebrows. Her eyes were the same faded blue-gray as her sister's.

"Hi!" Caroline said, glancing at her watch. "Did you close up early because of the storm?"

"No, no, no. Debbie works Sundays now. I told you that, didn't I?"

"I don't remember."

"Caroline, are you drunk?"

"A little."

"Well, slow down so I can catch up." Suzie grabbed

the beer out of her hand and finished it. "God, this place is crowded tonight!"

Henry zigzagged his way through the tables and sat next to Caroline. "Are we still on for tomorrow?" he asked Larry.

"I've got a new opening I want to try out," Larry said. Before leaving for the second shift, he played chess with Henry several afternoons a week.

Suzie Martello left after two beers, explaining that she had to open the store at five the next morning. By the time Pope stepped onstage, Caroline had drunk herself into a giggly state. She put her hand on Henry's shoulder and said, with the beginning of a slur, "Henry, Henry, when did you own this bar?"

"When did I what?"

"I told her you used to *own* this bar," Larry said, pantomiming playing a guitar behind Caroline's back.

Henry looked puzzled for a second, then broke into a wide grin. "Oh, that was a long time ago," he told her.

"Is that why you still get free drinks?" she asked.

"I suppose it is."

"It must be fun to own a bar."

Henry thought for a second. "It's a lot of work," he said, then he saw Rachel and her boyfriend walk in. He finished his drink in two quick gulps, said good night, and walked home.

Rachel had either turned off the hall light or it had burned out after she left, and the hall got darker the closer Henry came to his door at the end. He pulled his keys out of his pocket and bent forward, as if he were bowing, until his nose almost bumped the doorknob. He sucked hard on his cigarette to give himself enough light to find the keyhole.

Inside, once the overhead light was off and the lamp and the space heater were on, he hit the playback button on his phone machine. There were only two messages.

"Henry, this is Aaron. Dick just came in and said the snow has moved the deer down to the lower levels. There are tracks everywhere on Firespin, leading down to the orchard. If you come back up, there's a good chance. Dick didn't get a shot off but saw three just out of range, and I glassed one from the cabin down by the bridge. Give me a call if you can make it."

For over twenty years, during black powder season, Aaron had hosted a deer and bird hunt at his cabin in the White Mountains. And this was the last hunt. Aaron was sixty-one and dying of lung cancer. Too weak to hunt anymore, he had to content himself with his binoculars and his perch by the wood stove in front of the large picture windows that looked west down the fields and orchard toward Mount Carlisle.

Henry rewound the machine and played Aaron's message again, thinking of going back up. Like a filter, new snow changed everything in the woods, and sounds that might be missed before would now be clear. He imagined his iron sights framing a buck in the cold, failing light of evening and decided he'd try again.

He played the second message.

"Hey, Corvine, you bug. Your wife—excuse me, ex-wife—gave me this new number."

Henry recognized the voice.

"Listen," Tyler Beckett said, a little softer. "I didn't

even know about you and Kitty splitting up until last month, when I ran into Reynolds at the Bottom Line. But then again, I've had kind of a busy year. But you should've called me. I hope you're okay. Man, why on earth did you move back to Edson?" Then her voice got stronger again. "Listen, I have some business to discuss with you. It's very important. Call me tomorrow, okay? I'm at home. Off the road. Finally."

Henry rewound the machine and sat down on the bed, too tired to call. What sort of business? he wondered. It was typical of Tyler to be vague about that, about anything, and the familiarity of it made him smile. They hadn't talked in over a year, and he liked hearing her voice again. The last time, she called him in Laconia to say she'd just signed the deal with Seneca Records, a major label that had bought up the tiny independent Henry had been with. Her CD came out several months later, and Henry guessed that she'd spent the better part of the year promoting it on the road. He loved the advance cassette she had sent him the previous winter, but it wasn't until he heard his drunken skipper singing along with "Avenue C" on the jukebox, in the Dancing Leprechaun Topless Bar and Laundromat, that he realized how famous she had become.

POPE LED HER up the narrow stairway to his apartment, a quick walk down the hill from the Millhouse and across the street from the fire station. Her body sloshed from side to side against the walls. On the third-floor landing, she suddenly stopped and yanked Pope's hand, nearly pulling him on top of her. "My skis! Where're my skis?" Her mouth sounded like it was full of rubber bands.

"Shh," Pope whispered.

"My skis!" she shouted.

"It's all right, Caroline. We left 'em at the bar, remember?" He led her into the apartment. Taking off her parka, he draped it over a chair at the kitchen table, then covered it with his while she walked around the corner into the other room and sat down on his bed.

"Do y'all want anything to eat or some coffee or something?"

"I want a cigarette."

He looked around the corner. "You don't smoke."

"I want a cigarette. Please."

"All right." Pope took one from his shirt pocket, lit it and handed it to her, then walked back around the corner to the kitchen.

She heard the refrigerator door open. She pulled her sweater over her head, folded it, and set it on top of his chest of drawers. Pope cracked open a can of beer and joined her on the bed. He moved to unbuckle her belt, but she caught his wrist with her hand and held it against her. "Let me finish my cigarette first," she said. Pope set his beer down, walked to the record player, and played whatever was on the turntable. She didn't recognize it. When she stubbed out her cigarette, she unbuckled her belt and unsnapped her jeans.

Pope walked back to her. "Let me help," he said, kissing her lightly on the lips. She stood up unsteadily and unfastened her bra, while Pope knelt to remove her ski boots and her socks, then her jeans. When she was naked she crawled in under the covers, lay on her back, and stared at a corner of the ceiling. The room would not stay still. Shutting her eyes made her feel queasy, and she couldn't see one of anything with them open. Pope undressed and climbed in with her, kissed her and gently cupped one of her breasts in his hand. He moved his head down and kissed the nipple of the other breast. She sighed as his lips pulled on her. If she took particular pride in one part of her body, it was her breasts. Even Rachel had once remarked how she was all skin and bones except where it truly counted. Pope began to work his mouth down to her belly, her thighs. She squinted at the ceiling, wishing he would pay more attention to her breasts, but that wasn't what he wanted. She spread her legs a little more for him.

He was quick and soon he was off her, asleep with one arm draped over her chest. Still on her back, she closed both eyes and felt her stomach turn. Opening her eyes, she saw two ceiling corners. She squinted one eye again and stared at the single corner, somewhat stabilized and afraid to move. She stared at the corner for a long time before she could shut both eyes and fall asleep.

At six-thirty, the alarm went off and Pope slid out of bed. "I'll call you when I get off work. Let's do something tonight."

"Mmmnph," she answered. She could hear everything

in the tiny apartment—the whoosh of the gas flame under the coffeepot, the water hissing against the metal sides of the shower, his footsteps, dresser drawers carefully pulled out, and, finally, the click of the door shutting and boots clunking down the stairs. She fell back asleep.

She woke again at ten o'clock. Pope had left the aspirin bottle out on the kitchen table. She swallowed three, turned the gas burner on under the pot, and lit one of Pope's half-smoked cigarette butts. Then she walked into the other room and saw her ski boots. My God! she thought. My skis! She searched the apartment, but they weren't there. When the coffee started to boil, she turned off the gas and poured a cup and took it into the other room. She would have to call Pope at the gas station about her skis.

The apartment was warm, and she sat down on the braided rug in front of his record collection. This was the first time she'd ever been alone in his apartment. The other nights she'd stayed over were on the weekend, when he didn't have to work in the morning. She wanted to hear something gentle while she sipped her coffee and woke up. She wanted to hear Mississippi John Hurt. Pope played him all the time, and she loved his soft, warm voice. It didn't matter that she could understand only half the words; she just liked the way he sounded. He wasn't like the other blues singers Pope listened to. They sounded too harsh and grating, their rhythms sometimes herky-jerky, as if they couldn't keep a beat. She fanned through the records, looking for a John Hurt album that had a gray cover. She pulled out jacket after jacket, but nothing was in order and she'd never seen or heard many of the records. She saw one that was the right color and pulled it out, but it wasn't Mississippi John Hurt. The album was called *The River and the Mill,* and it was by Henry Corvine. Her fingers jerked, and the jacket landed faceup on the floor. Her neighbor Henry looked up at her in black and white. In the picture his hair was a little longer and he hadn't shaved; he looked younger too, though she thought he still looked young. The cover was signed *To Eloise. All the best, Henry.* Eloise, she knew, was Pope's sister. She got up, carrying the record, and searched the apartment for the remnants of another cigarette, glancing at the cover photograph between ashtrays. In the kitchen she finally found a long butt, straightened and lit it, then returned to the other room. She stared at the cover for a long time before she put the record on. When the needle dropped to the record, the first thing she heard were the scratches. This record had been played a lot. But Caroline felt she was doing something wrong, like reading someone's diary, and might get caught.

The opening song, "River Beyond the Bridge," was the one Pope had sung that first night at the Millhouse, about the millworker walking home from work. The scratches continued through the guitar introduction, then the vocal came on, and she gasped as she heard Pope singing, only the voice was lower, rougher. She turned the frayed jacket over and looked again at Henry's picture. Judging by its worn condition, she guessed the record was at least ten years old. How could Henry, if that was Henry singing, record one of Pope's songs so long ago? Was

Pope that good as a teenager? Pope had told her that he'd met Henry when he was only fourteen. How could Henry sound so much like him? He had all of Pope's quirky vocal mannerisms—the growling way of accenting certain words, half talking the song. She ground out the smoldering filter as she read the credits on the back of the jacket: *All songs written by Henry Corvine. Published by Yorikke Music, BMI* © *1980, 1981.* All the times she heard Pope perform "River Beyond the Bridge," he'd never claimed to have written it, but she didn't like it that he'd neglected to say who had.

Caroline finished her coffee and played the entire album, moving only to flip the record over. It was like listening to a Pope Johnson set, but sometimes her whole body shivered as she heard certain catches and realized it wasn't Pope but Henry who was singing.

She listened to the record twice, then looked around the apartment for a blank cassette, but she couldn't find one in Pope's pile of tapes. She considered just taking the record and making a copy at home, then decided not to because she didn't have a key and couldn't return without Pope knowing about it. She didn't understand why he'd never mentioned Henry's record, or why Henry never said anything about being a musician. After making the bed, she put the record away and left Pope a bland little note on the kitchen table.

Outside, the piercing noon sunlight brought her headache back. She stopped to buy a blank cassette at Martello's. Suzie told her she didn't look well at all and should go home to bed.

AT NOON Larry banged on Henry's door. "Hey, Henry! It's almost noon. Let's push wood," he shouted.

"Fuck chess," Henry muttered, waking with a start. "Yo, Larry, I just woke up," he called from the bed. "I'll be over in a couple minutes."

"Cappuccino?"

"Yeah, a double," Henry shouted. Larry's one positive New York experience was acquiring an espresso machine.

"You got it."

Henry sat up and lit a cigarette, then pulled on his dungarees and turned on the radio. It was the country station. He didn't like the song but kept the radio on in case the next one was better. He finished dressing and sat down at the phone, looked up a number in his book, and dialed.

"Tyler Beckett's office. Lizzie speaking."

"Hey, Lizzie. This is Henry Corvine." He'd known Lizzie as a singer, before she'd become Tyler's assistant. "Is Tyler around?"

"Oh, Henry, hi! She'll be so glad you called, but you just missed her. She needs to see you, though. How soon can you get down here?"

"Down there? New York? No, no, I don't think so." He wasn't awake and felt his thoughts were being pushed through molasses.

"No, you don't understand," she said. "Tyler needs to see you."

"I'd like to see her too, but I don't go to New York. She knows that."

"What do you mean, you don't go to New York?"

"I don't go to New York," he said. "It's that simple. I'd rather eat linoleum than go to New York City."

"You don't understand." She said it distinctly and slowly this time. "Tyler Beckett has some business to discuss with you, and it's urgent."

Henry did understand, and he didn't want to speak to this woman who had proudly not been off the island of Manhattan in seven years. "I'll be here if she needs to talk."

"Don't you even want to know what it's about?"

"If it's important, I suppose I'll find out soon enough."

"All right," she said, and Henry detected the tone of a person who was about to blame all her frustrations and failures on his refusal. "I'll tell her you won't come to New York. Is that what you want?" This sounded nasty, like a threat, and it woke Henry up.

"No," Henry said. "Tell her I returned her call and she can call me when she gets in. I should be around today and for the first part of this week. *That's* what I want. Do *you* understand?"

There was silence on the other end of the line.

"Do you understand?" he said again, insistent.

"I'll give her your message."

"Damn right you will," he said, hanging up.

He thought how much he wanted to see Tyler again,

and how much he hated and feared New York. Even thinking about it made his stomach knot up. The more time he
spent there, the less he understood the city; and the less
he understood it, the more it terrified him. He remembered
joking with Tyler over the phone that New York had its
own rulebook and he'd gotten a bad translation. Still, he
wanted to see her again. Years ago, they'd go drink in
Village clubs until four in the morning, talking music and
songwriting and more music. Once, she showed him some
new lyrics in her notebook and asked what he thought the
music should be like. He'd paused, then said, "Well, these
look like polka lyrics to me." She'd punched him on the
shoulder and called him a peckerwood.

He dialed Aaron's number and worried when no one
answered. Aaron should be in the cabin, but maybe he was
taking a shower or a nap. Henry decided to call again in
an hour, then went down the hall to play chess with Larry.

Except for the furnishings, Larry's apartment was a
mirror image of Rachel and Caroline's. There was a leg-
less, threadbare couch against the wall that faced the television and stereo, and a worn easy chair next to the couch.
A wooden industrial spool served as a coffee table. Two
walls were filled from floor to ceiling with books, mostly
fiction and ornithology, some poetry, chess, history, and a
few odd editions ranging from sexuality to British comedy.
On another wall he had tacked up a poster tracing the
evolution of mankind from ape and earliest caveman to
Homo erectus, and on a table beneath it he'd arranged a
line of Chia Pets in progressive stages of development.
Above the couch was an Audubon study of a woodcock.

Larry let Henry in, and he took his usual seat at the kitchen table. A steaming cappuccino waited for him beside the chessboard, and Larry was making a cup for himself. Nailed to the wall above his head was a framed and signed photograph of Bernie Carbo in his Red Sox uniform—one of Larry's yard sale finds. "I think I got a little drunk last night," he said.

"I've found the more I drink," Henry said, "the smarter I get."

"The more I drink, the more irresistible I become to women."

"Caroline looked like she was doing okay for herself too last night, didn't she?"

Larry laughed. "Oh, you left a little too early."

"She take that express train all the way to Smartsville?"

"Got elected mayor."

"She get home okay?"

"Yeah, sort of," Larry said, steaming the milk for his cappuccino. "Pope took care of her." He brought his cup to the table and sat down, emptied the ceramic ashtray into the wastebasket behind his chair, and set it beside the chessboard. "Well, let's see what's going on around the seacoast today," he said, turning on his scanner—a Radio Shack 2005 he'd modified by clipping a diode so he could pick up cellular phone calls from as far away as Seabrook. But the scanner was quiet. "This thing's always more fun," he said, "late at night when the bars close."

"You'll get arrested with that thing someday," Henry said.

"Hey, you used to write down whole conversations going on in the next booth in the bar and then turn 'em into songs. It's the same thing, only I don't write it down. You wouldn't believe some of the things I hear."

"Do you ever recognize voices?"

"Sure," Larry said. "Sometimes I know who it is."

"So what's this new opening you were talking about last night?"

"This thing I read about called the Danish Gambit." Larry lit a cigarette. "I really don't know what I'm doing with it. It seems kind of suicidal to me."

"Well, how's it go?"

"I basically give you three pawns at the opening, in return for superior position. I mean, you've got to accept the gambit, of course. Humor me for the first five moves."

"Sure."

They played until two-thirty, when Larry had to leave for work. At first the gambit had appeared as illogical as it sounded, as Henry's pawns quickly tore through Larry's front line. But that only freed Larry up to develop his bishops and control the center of the board. When they adjourned for the day, Henry was still a piece up but was playing defensively.

Back in his apartment, he called Aaron again.

"Was that you who called around noon?" Aaron asked.

"Yeah."

"I thought it might be. I was outside helping Perry skin his buck."

"Really? What'd he get?"

"A nice four-pointer," Aaron said.

"How about Dick?"

"He's still out. Are you coming back up?"

"Yeah, I should be up there around Thursday, maybe Wednesday night."

"I'll be here."

"Thanks." Henry hung up. He took the two partridge out of the refrigerator, plucked and cleaned them, then put them back. He washed his hands, zipped up his hooded sweatshirt with the jellyfish stains still on it, slipped on his leather jacket, and started down the stairs. As always at that time of day, Crazy Betty sat in the lobby facing Main Street, wearing a blue housecoat and faded pink slippers. Her hair was greasy and thin enough to show the outline of her skull. She saw Henry and screeched, "Do gotta digarette?" Her voice sounded like air brakes. She already had a cigarette in her hand, one of Larry's Camel Lights, but Henry reached into his breast pocket and gave her the last Merit in the pack.

Outside, it was warm and the snow was melting in the bright sunlight. Henry walked down to Main Street and stopped at Martello's for another pack of Merits. He still had more than half a pack of Kool Milds in his jacket from the night before. Suzie and Debbie were working behind the counter with their mother.

"How're you feeling today, Henry?" Suzie asked.

"I'm fine," he said, puzzled. "Why?"

"Caroline was in here around noon and she looked like hell. Wicked hung over."

"I guess she did a little drinking last night. I left early myself." He paid for his cigarettes and turned to leave.

Suzie said, "Henry?" and by her tone he knew she was going to ask him for a favor.

"Yeah?"

She walked around the counter to a shelf of baked goods and snacks and handed him two packages of Hostess cupcakes. "Would you take these up to Caroline for me? They're her favorites, and I can't leave the store."

"I just left the Prescott," he said. "I'm on my way out."

"Please."

"I'll pick them up on my way back," he said.

"When'll that be?"

"Couple hours. I don't know."

"Well, just take them," she insisted.

"I'm not walking around all day with cupcakes in my pockets."

"But I don't get off work until five."

"I'll pick them up later. I've got to go."

"Don't forget," she said.

"I'll see you later."

On the sidewalk outside, Louis Martineau was directing the road crew as they cleaned up the downed branches and uncovered sewer grates to drain the water backing up and flooding the lower parts of Main Street. He wore a beige cowboy hat Henry had never seen before. Cowboy hats themselves were a rarity in New Hampshire, where there wasn't much need for them. Martineau pushed up the front brim of his hat with his index finger while he barked out orders. Henry laughed to himself. He might just as well have been wearing a fez.

Water rained down from the gutters above the shops. The whole town was wet and sloppy and sunny, and Henry felt happy to be there. He unzipped his sweatshirt as he worked his way through and around groups of people standing in front of the shops, smoking and talking, waiting for their shift to begin. He bumped into Larry coming out of Judy's Lunch. Larry had the Manchester *Union Leader* and the Boston *Globe* tucked under his arm.

"What a day, eh?" Henry said, affecting a clipped French-Canadian accent.

"Fuckin', eh?" Larry returned. "Hey, there's something I forgot to ask you earlier. What's your shoe size?"

"My shoe size? A nine. Why?"

"Just curious," Larry said.

Henry screwed up his face and cocked his head, then said so long and continued down the street, passing a narrow yellow apartment building where he'd once lived. Four stories high, it sagged in the middle—almost banana-shaped—and was commonly referred to as the Tiltin' Hilton. Henry was surprised to find it still standing when he moved back to town.

A murder of crows clung to the power lines above him like a football team in formation, ready to scrimmage against nobody.

He walked down to the Gulf station where Pope worked. Henry felt like shooting pool at the Polish Club, and Pope was the only person he could think of who was free at that time. They were fairly evenly matched, and Henry liked him better when what they were doing was not even remotely connected to music. Pope was sitting on a bench in the office, playing a cheap, nylon-string guitar somebody had left behind long before. Once a full-service station with two bays and two mechanics, now this was just a gas station, and nobody fixed flats or adjusted timing. In a few minutes, when the first shift let out, business would get brisk, but by then Pope's shift would be over. Henry walked in and picked up the Louisville Slugger they kept under the counter, took a few false swings, and set it back down. In warmer weather he used to take it around the back of the station and knock gravel and small rocks in the direction of the railroad tracks. "Where's Bruce?" he asked. Bruce worked the next shift.

"Who knows?"

"Well, after he gets here, are you up for some eight-ball at the Polish Club?"

"Can't today." Two cars pulled up to the pumps. Pope passed the guitar to Henry as he got up. "How 'bout tomorrow?"

"Yeah, maybe." Henry set the guitar on the counter and followed Pope outside. He handled one pump while Pope took the other. "I think I'm going back up to the mountain, maybe Wednesday or Thursday."

"Good luck, then. Hey, you know, I'm serious about moving to New York. I haven't given my notice or anything yet, but this is an easy job if you want it. I'm sure you could get it. I ain't told a soul yet. You should call Dick Savage."

"I might." Henry figured that if he was waiting in line for the job, Pope wouldn't have to give any notice and could relocate anytime he wanted. It wasn't an entirely generous offer, but at the same time Henry thought he might like working at the station for a while. An easy job, no pressure, mostly slow-paced. He could walk to work and wouldn't have to make any serious plans for the future. It didn't pay much, but his expenses were so low he'd be able to put a little money away each week.

As he walked back through town, one of the mailmen, Jack Tilly, passed him in his truck and gave Henry a little wave, pointing at him with his index and middle finger on top of each other like the barrels of a shotgun. Jack played bass in a bluegrass band, and Henry had known him for years. He returned the wave.

Pumping gas wouldn't be his life's work, he thought, but it could be all right for a while.

SHE WAS AWAKE when her mother called, but still in bed at three-forty in the afternoon.

"Caroline?"

"Hi, Mom." She'd been lying on her back, waiting while her headache slowly faded. "What's up?"

"I just wanted to know if you're bringing anybody to dinner tonight?"

Dinner? she thought. Oh, my God, it's Monday! Dinner at her parents' house with Father Heire. With the early snow and getting drunk and Pope and the hangover, she'd forgotten all about it. "No, Mom," she said. "I'm coming by myself. What time is it?"

"Six o'clock," her mother said hesitantly. Dinner was always at six.

"Do you need any help?" Caroline sat up in bed and held her forehead.

"It's a little late for that, dear, but thanks for asking."

"Okay, see you later." She hung up, and as she swung her legs onto the floor, the phone rang again. "Hi," she said.

This time it was Pope. "I only got off work now."

She looked at the clock again. "What happened?"

"Bruce was late."

"Again?"

"He just showed up. Can you believe it? That's the third time in two weeks he pulled this shit. So you wanna do something tonight?"

"Oh, Pope, I can't. I have to have dinner with my folks." She thought he might be angry, but he persisted.

"Can't you bag it this one time?" he said. "Tell them you're sick or something? It's not like you never see them."

"I can't. I have to go. Father Heire's coming. We have him over for dinner once a month, and we're all expected to be there."

"But you don't live at home anymore," he said. "You have your own life. You gonna go to dinner there once a month when you're forty?"

"Pope, I don't know. I just have to go. I'm sorry. I'd rather be with you."

"And you're working all week?"

"Always do."

"But I really want to see you tonight," he said. "I was thinking about you all day."

"And I want to see you, but I just can't tonight." She knew, though, that as soon as she hung up he'd call someone else.

"Well, come by the station and visit me on your way to work tomorrow."

She didn't like that idea. A lot of girls dropped by the station, to help him pump gas, to listen to him play guitar. That was the thing about Pope, she thought. People did things for him. They pumped his gas, gave him rides, lined up gigs, fed him, bought him drinks, went to bed with him. At times he seemed so helpless that nothing would ever happen unless someone stepped in, and someone usually did.

There was a knock on the front door.

"Look, I've got to go," she said, exasperated. "Somebody's at the door. Call me later in the week?" She didn't mean to make it sound like a question.

"Of course. You take care."

"Oh—Pope!" she added. "Where are my skis?"

"They're up at the Millhouse, Caroline."

"Thanks. Bye." She put on her bathrobe and answered the door. Henry was standing in the hall with Hostess cupcakes in each extended hand. "Hey," he said. "Special delivery, Edson style."

"Oh, my God! My favorite. How'd you know?" she said, taking the packages from him. "Come on in. You want some coffee?"

"No, thanks," he said, stepping inside. "Suzie asked

me to give them to you. And this." He held out a box of Alka-Seltzer.

"Oh, Henry, that's so nice of you. Want a beer or something?"

"No, no. I'm all set," he said. "You relax."

She pulled her robe tighter. "Was I awful last night?"

"No, you were fine. It's no big deal, believe me." He didn't really know how drunk she'd been. "I've been ten times worse. Twenty times."

Rachel breezed in through the open door. "Well, look at you two. And you in your robe. I'm not interrupting anything, am I?"

"Just my hangover," Caroline said.

"I went over to the mall," Rachel said. "Look what I bought." She reached into her shopping bag, brought out a black merry widow, and held it up against her body. "Isn't this cool? Look, garters and everything. And . . ." She reached back into the bag and pulled out several packages of black stockings and a tiny matching G-string.

"Caroline," Henry said, inspecting the G-string and sliding into a croaky, north woods accent. "Looks like Rachel's been shoppin' over to Freeport, Christsake. You know, I'm partial to them crotchless down vests, myself. Wicked sexy. Puts the thrill right back into hiking."

Rachel snatched the G-string out of his hands. "Do you want me to, like, model these for you, Henry?" She batted her eyelashes and rocked her hips side to side slightly. He started to feel aroused, but before he could answer, she laughed and said, "In your dreams!" She dropped everything back in her shopping bag and disappeared into her room.

"I think Rachel's home," Henry said. They both laughed a little uneasily. "Look, I better go. I hope you feel better."

"Henry, thanks for bringing that stuff, especially the Alka-Seltzer."

"Yeah, uh, listen, I think I'm going back up to hunt, maybe Wednesday," he said. "I may be gone a couple days."

"You want me to pick up your mail?"

"Yeah, would you?"

"Of course," she said. He started to leave, then she said, "Henry?"

He stopped at the door. "Yeah?"

"I heard your record this morning. At Pope's."

"Oh? Which one?"

"*The River and the Mill*. How many do you have?"

"Three, more or less."

"More or less?"

"It's a long, stupid story. Only two were released."

"I just wanted to tell you how much I loved it," she said. "It's incredible! You're so good. I played it through twice, back to back. Where can I get it—and the others?"

"You can't. They're out of print."

"Don't you have any copies?"

"No." All his copies were in boxes up in Laconia with his ex-wife. He turned to leave.

She put her hand on his arm. "I know where Pope gets it all from." As she spoke, she felt an anger building inside her; it was some form of stealing on Pope's part, she knew, but it was different from a little girl pocketing a candy bar at Martello's or somebody robbing a bank. Pope was stealing something that couldn't be touched or tasted or spent. Maybe it's closer to lying, she thought, but it was just as wrong as stealing. She couldn't understand why Henry acted as if nothing was wrong.

Henry smiled, but the smile looked like it came from a thousand miles away. Then she saw his jaw was set.

"I have to go," he said.

She closed the door behind him and listened while he walked the few steps to his door. She heard his key click into the lock, heard the door open and shut. Then she knocked on Rachel's door and walked in, still confused and angry. Dressed in her merry widow, stockings, G-string, and heels, Rachel was turning herself back and forth in front of her mirror.

"What do you think?" she said to Caroline. "Isn't this cool?"

"I think you were teasing Henry again."

"Jesus fucking Christ, Caroline! What's the matter with you? The man's, like, what—forty? He knows I'd never go out with somebody that old. What the hell would we do—go to a Sally Fields film festival?"

"Shh!" she said, knowing Henry could hear them through the walls.

"Yeah, right," Rachel said, a little softer. "Look, I'm not leading the guy on. He knows what's going on. I'm just having a little fun. He enjoys it too. Don't think he doesn't. Come on, it's all just a game, a little play."

Caroline said nothing. Maybe it *was* some sort of game, one she didn't understand but that Rachel could play at the master level. She watched Rachel admiring herself in the mirror. "Do you think guys really like women dressed up like that in bed?"

"All guys are different," Rachel said. "I had a boyfriend once who couldn't perform unless I talked dirty to him."

"Really? What did you do?"

"I talked dirty to him, and the sex was great. When I did what he wanted he got so hard! You just do it. It's not like people get to choose what turns them on or not. That just happens to you. It's nothing to be embarrassed about. I just want to take the initiative on this date tonight. I think most guys like sexy underwear. I really think we should stop at the mall tomorrow on the way to work and pick out something sexy for you. I bet it would really turn Pope on."

"I wouldn't know what to get," Caroline said.

"Well, I'd help you," Rachel said. "Or we could ask Henry. He's been around the block a couple times."

"Henry?" She didn't want that. "No."

"Yeah, that's perfect. Henry would have some good ideas. He's an older guy." She picked up her phone and dialed as Caroline protested. "Henry," Rachel said. "Caroline and I need your advice, a man's perspective. Can you come over? It'll only take a second. . . . Great."

She hung up the phone and slipped a short silk kimono over her lingerie. She took three lingerie catalogs from the top of her chest of drawers and led Caroline out to the divan in the living room. When Henry knocked, Rachel let him in and sat him down next to Caroline. "Caroline wants you, as a man, to help her pick out something sexy for her. Do you want a beer?"

"Are you serious?" he asked Caroline, whose face suddenly reddened.

Before she could answer, Rachel said, "Sure, we're serious. Do you want a beer?"

"All right. But why me?"

"Because you're a man. At least that's the rumor going around. And women wear things like this for men, not for themselves, for Godsake! Now look through these catalogs and find something for Caroline." She got up to get Henry a beer.

"Okay." He looked at Caroline staring at the catalogs in front of him, her face burning. She wouldn't look at him. He started flipping pages. He knew she was uncomfortable and wanted him to pick out something safe, something feminine but not sleazy. "This is pretty," he said, pointing to a model in a print chemise and wrap.

"Yeah, right. I think my *grandmother* has something like that," Rachel said, handing Henry his beer and sitting next to him. The hem of her kimono rode up above her stockings. She ignored it. "We want sexy, not pretty."

Caroline caught Henry glancing at Rachel's garter belt.

"We want hot, steamy, 'Fuck me, take me, Henry.' Not 'The kids are asleep. Wanna do it?' Find something that turns you on."

"Anything in these catalogs made of sheepskin or wool?" he asked.

"I'm serious, Henry." Rachel turned several pages, then tapped a fingertip on a picture of a model in a sheer black baby doll. "What about this? Does this turn you on? It would really showcase her breasts, don't you think?"

"Oh, God!" Caroline said, looking away.

"It's good," he said. "Very sexy." He looked at Caroline. "You'd look killer in this, but let's see what else they have." He took a sip of beer and thumbed through more pages.

"Henry," Rachel said, "think of it like you and Caroline are lovers and you're picking out something special for her to wear, you know, the first time."

"Maybe we shouldn't be doing this," Caroline said.

"*This* is really sexy," Henry said, pointing to a model in what was described as "a sheer spaghetti-strapped, suspender catsuit." "You'd look incredible in this, Caroline."

Before she could say anything, Rachel interjected, "And there's a store at the mall that has something just like that!"

"I don't know," Caroline said.

"No way. We're getting this for you tomorrow." Rachel let the kimono ride farther up her thigh.

"Caroline," Henry said, "just buy what you feel good about. I like this, but some other guy might have a completely different choice."

"But does it turn you on, Henry?" Rachel said coyly. "Are you getting excited?"

"You asked for my opinion," Henry told her. "I think Caroline would look great in this outfit. That's all I can say." He finished his beer and set down the can.

Caroline watched Rachel as she shifted her position on the divan, revealing the lace top of her merry widow.

"Well, that settles it, then. Caroline, we'll get you something just like this."

"You need me for anything else?" Henry asked, standing up.

"No, that's it," Rachel said. "Thanks, Henry." After he left she said, "Caroline, we'll stop on the way to work."

Caroline wondered if Pope would like her to dress up like that, and if any of the other girls he slept with did. Mostly she wanted to have a nap before she had to leave for supper.

"Come in here a minute," Rachel said, taking her into the bedroom. She pulled two dresses from her closet, one black and the other navy. "Which one?" she said, holding them up.

"Why are you going through all this for Roger? You don't even like him all that much."

"I'm not going out with Roger tonight," Rachel said, then paused. "I'm having dinner in Boston with Lionel Tanner." She tilted her head and smiled triumphantly.

"Oh, my God!"

"That's what I said."

"No wonder you're getting so dressed up. He's gorgeous!"

"And he owns the whole damn mill," Rachel added. "Or at least his family does. So which dress?"

"The navy one's classier."

"You're right." She put the black dress back in the closet.

Caroline asked, "Do you really think Pope would like that outfit on me? What if he laughs?"

"Believe me, he wouldn't laugh at you. With your tits, you'd be unstoppable. Could I borrow your pearls tonight? *Please?*"

"Okay," Caroline said, then went back to bed for another hour.

HENRY ATE a baloney sandwich while he looked for a new partridge recipe in his game cookbook. Everything required too many ingredients, so he decided on his old tarragon and butter standby. He had everything he needed in the cupboard. He closed the cookbook and put it away.

Putting his jacket on, he walked down the back stairs to the parking lot to shovel out his car. He opened the trunk for the snow shovel he kept there year round and started to work. The snow was wet and heavy now. Though other cars flanked him and had prevented the plows from socking him in, there was still plenty to shovel out around the rear bumper. He thought of Pope Johnson as he worked, wishing that Caroline hadn't brought him up. At the same time, he was pleased she'd understood, however incompletely, that Pope had picked him clean and pasted his own name on everything Henry had spent years learning and developing. Strangely, he'd been flattered the first time he heard Pope play. And he knew Pope couldn't have taken what he had if Henry were still performing. But he wasn't, so anything he'd done was, in a way, fair game.

By the time he'd cleared the bumpers, he was out of breath and sweating. Up in his apartment, he lay down and tried to fall asleep but couldn't. Only a few older critics and fans, he realized, would even notice what Pope was doing. When he finally got up it was dark, and the lights from the parking lot had come on. Maybe he had slept for a little while.

Except for the baloney sandwich, he hadn't eaten all day and now was hungry. He decided to save the partridge; it would take too long to prepare and cook, and partridge was better after it had aged a few days. He decided to go to the Polish Club, where he could get a couple slices of microwaved pizza.

THE COLD FRONT returned that night. A skin of polished black ice covered the roads, invisible except under streetlights and headlights. Caroline hid the bottom half of her face in her scarf as she hurried along the sidewalk to her parents' house. They lived a block away from the Our Lady of the Immaculate Conception church, where she'd been baptized and confirmed. To keep her balance, she slid her boots over the sidewalk as if she were skiing. At least her parents' driveway would be plowed, sanded, and salted. Her younger brother, Stephen, would've taken care of that the night before. Harold, her older brother, would've opened another beer and complained about it while he waited for Stephen to start. "Hey," he always said, "I did my share of the shoveling when you were too small."

The streets here in Polishtown were arranged in a grid—the only part of Edson where anything could be found at right angles. The small, asbestos-shingled houses had originally been identical. When the immigrants arrived from Czwykla, the church and the mill split construction costs and served together as landlord. Once the worker's rent had paid off the mortgage on each house, the Tanner Company bought out the church and began selling the houses. Though it was no longer exclusively Polish, it would always be Polishtown.

Caroline walked up the three cement steps and pushed open the front door. Stephen sat in the living room, watching the news on television. At first the air inside felt warm, but as she hung up her coat in the hall it seemed to turn thick and heavy, filled with the familiar smells of a roast in the oven and boiling vegetables. Her mother boiled her vegetables until they were so limp and pasty that only the faintest hint of taste remained, something Caroline had never noticed until she moved out of the house.

"Hi," she said to Stephen on her way to the kitchen. "Nice job on the driveway," she added over her shoulder. Engrossed, he waved hello distractedly.

Her mother bounced around the kitchen from stove to cabinet to refrigerator, then shot past Caroline like an electron breaking free. From the dining room she called, "Will you check the vegetables for me, honey?"

There was one pot on the stove with potatoes and

another with string beans. Steam was rattling the covers, and Caroline hoped she wasn't too late. She turned both burners to low, picked up a fork, and poked the potatoes. They still felt firm, but the string beans were as flaccid as shoelaces.

Her mother hurried back to the kitchen. "I'm running so late!" she said breathlessly. She took a lead-glass pitcher from the cupboard, set it on the counter, and began cracking trays of ice into it.

Caroline took the tray from her hand. "You go get ready, Mom. I can take over from here."

"Father Heire will be here in twenty minutes!"

"I've *got* it, Mom."

"The table's all set except for the water. Just keep an eye on the vegetables and the roast."

"Go!" Caroline ordered.

"All right, I'm going, I'm going." Her mother kissed her on the forehead and rushed off to the bedroom.

The kitchen windows were opaque with steam, and Caroline suddenly felt a little faint as she turned off the string beans, filled the pitcher with ice water, and put it on the dining room table. She wanted a cigarette. She wanted to be home in bed. The yellowish ceiling light and the steamy windows made the kitchen seem small and dingy, though she knew her mother kept the house spotless. She opened the oven to check the roast.

Harold walked in, took a beer from the refrigerator, and sat down at the kitchen table. "Hi, kid. When'd you get in?"

"Just a minute ago," she said. Harold was wearing a

clean blue button-down shirt and pressed blue Dickies. His hair was still damp from the shower. "You look nice," Caroline said.

He cracked his beer. "What's new?"

"Not much."

"You still seeing Leo Filion?" He leaned forward, his belly swelling over his belt enough to hide the buckle. It was the only fat he had on him. His face was tight and firm, his arms wiry and strong, and his spindly legs some-how supported everything like a golf tee.

"No," she said.

"Good. I ran into him down to the Eagles last week-end. He quit Grossman's, you know."

"Oh?"

"That's right." He took a long drink from the can, then combed a bit of foam out of his mustache with his index finger. "He got himself a job down to the navy yard. Apprentice welder or some such. Thinks he's on the fast track now." He laughed.

"Well, good for him."

"I never liked him."

"Well, the navy yard should pay better than Gross-man's."

"Maybe. But there's lots of people think it's just a matter of time before the government shuts it down. Hell, I could've taken a job down there two months ago myself, and it did pay better, but there was no guarantee the job would still be around a year from now, and then what would I do? Nah, I'll stay at the mill. It's not the greatest job, but it's not the worst either. And hell, that mill's been

around forever. And like Dad says, people are always going to need shoes."

As if on cue, Caroline's father walked into the kitchen.
He took a beer from the refrigerator, let Caroline kiss him
on the cheek, and sat down across from Harold. He'd come
up from his workshop down in the cellar, and he smelled
of gun oil and the sweet scent of Hoppe's No. 9. He
couldn't have done much work on his guns, since he was
already dressed for dinner. Just wiping them down, she
thought, or running a patch through his deer rifle, a Marlin
.35. She had impressed Henry, the first time she'd visited
his apartment to drop off his mail, by complimenting him
on his Ruger International .308. Harold had once owned
the same model, but sold it to make the down payment on
a used pickup. That weekend or the next, her father would
go out with her uncle Freddy and try his luck around the
Connecticut River Valley. He came home with a deer more
often than not, and Caroline loved venison.

He wore a blue shirt identical to Harold's, under the
sport jacket Caroline's mother always made him wear when
Father Heire came to dinner. He crossed his legs and
opened his beer. "I overheard that last part," he said.
"Harold's right. On one hand, you never know what the
government is going to do—and neither do they, for Godsake. On the other hand, people need shoes and always
will. There might come a time when we don't need sub-
marines, but we're sure gonna need shoes. And Tanner
shoes are top quality, the best. I could still get you that
job in the Tanner offices, Caroline, if you want. You're
good at that paperwork—always were, just like your

mother. You can't be a waitress your whole life." He scratched at his sideburns, which were a little darker than the graying hair on his temples and flared out at his jawline like the bell of a clarinet.

Caroline looked at the kitchen clock. In ten minutes Father Heire would arrive. He was always punctual with everything, from Masses to appointments to dinner engagements. "I'd better open the wine," she said, excusing herself to the dining room. The only time they drank wine was when Father Heire came to dinner.

NAPPY BAUDETTE made the eight ball in the side pocket but scratched in the corner with the cue, losing the game. Henry saw it was a scratch before the shot but kept quiet. Nappy asked what he was drinking.

"I'll have another Molson." He burped and tasted pizza again.

The Polish Club was filling up with the after-supper crowd, people taking their usual seats, ordering their usual drinks, playing cards or Ping-Pong or shooting pool, some just waiting for Monday Night Football to start. Henry sat down at his table and picked at the beer nuts spilled out of their bag around his empty beer bottle. Nappy Baudette returned with a Budweiser for himself and a fresh Molson for Henry. "You get your deer yet?" he asked.

"Not yet," Henry said. "I'm going back up, though."

"You hunt up to Mount Carlisle, right?" Nappy said. "My cousin works for IPC in Bristol. I fished up there last spring."

"You fish the Newfound?"

"Yup."

"How'd you do?"

"Did okay."

"Pretty stretch of river there, coming off the lake."

"Yup. Wish there was more of it."

Nappy Baudette weighed nearly three hundred pounds. He worked the first shift at the mill and had been shooting pool at the Polish Club since his shift let out at three. The soft, round fingers of his left hand were powdered white with chalk and looked like crullers. He moved in graceful slow motion, like something in still water, and was delicate with the cue stick, never using more force than was required to sink a ball and line the cue ball up for the next shot. "Want to play for a couple bucks, Henry?" he asked. "Nothing big, just a buck or two a game, maybe five?"

"Come on, Nappy, you know I don't play for money," Henry said. "Beers are enough for me."

"Beers it is, then," Nappy said. He racked the balls. "Your break."

Henry stood up with his cue stick, scooped some beer nuts off the Formica tabletop, and washed them down with his new Molson. He broke the rack and sank a low ball.

During his first summer in Alaska years ago, he'd shot pool regularly and learned to control the cue ball and use the pips to work out his angles. He quickly discovered that in Ketchikan there was little to do except fish, drink, read,

talk, and shoot pool—and that no matter how many show-
ers he took or how much deodorant he used, he'd still
smell like fish and none of the women on the tourist boats
would have anything to do with him. So he and McManus
drank and read and shot pool whenever they had time off.

Their favorite place was the Dancing Leprechaun Topless Bar and Laundromat, where they could shoot rack
after rack of eight-ball or nine-ball and drink while they
washed a load of cold, salty laundry and watched the strip-
pers dance to the music on the jukebox. Each stripper
would feed a quarter into the juke, climb up on a tiny
stage, then dance the first song with her top on and the
second with her top off. Then she'd refasten her top, pick
up her tray, and wait tables while another waitress fed a
quarter into a jukebox, in a kind of tag-team procession.
When Henry and McManus got tired of pool, they sometimes dropped by the Toucan 69. The waitresses were
prostitutes up from Texas for the fishing season and the
fishermen's money. Henry never went there as a john, and
liked to call himself a window shopper. Once the waitresses at the Toucan got to know them, since McManus
was from Austin, they often drank for nothing at the end
of the night.

Henry had never liked to wager on sports or tricks,
and it was at the Leprechaun that he made his last money
bet. One night after he and McManus had put down their
cue sticks and ordered one last round, two drunken deck-
hands approached their table. One said, "I'll bet you
guys fifty bucks that my friend here can chug down two
schooners of beer while standing on his head."

McManus looked at Henry. "I don't think he can even stand on his feet. Let's do it."

Henry recognized the second man, the drinker, from Beaufort. He was the skiffman on the *Rendezvous*. They called him Sluice, and Henry didn't know any other name for him. "Fifty bucks apiece or together?"

"Either way," the arbitrator said.

Sluice leaned heavily against a post with his hands in his pockets, his eyes glazed and his face without expression.

"Let's go fifty bucks together," Henry said to McManus.

"No, fifty each," McManus whispered. "He's already weaving drunk. Besides, you can't chug a beer when you're upside down. It's physically impossible. Fifty bucks, okay?"

"All right," Henry said, knowing he was also a little drunk and that fifty dollars was almost all the money he had on him.

"Fifty bucks for each of us," McManus said. "Let's see your money and we'll buy the beer."

The first drunk pulled the bills from his shirt pocket and laid them on the table. Henry and McManus followed suit and ordered two drafts from the waitress. When she brought them, Sluice set the schooners on the floor beside the post he'd been leaning against, then bent down and kicked into a headstand, wrapping his legs around the post. He reached for the first beer and drained it. McManus took a camera from his jacket pocket and squeezed off three quick shots. Henry half expected to see Sluice's nostrils spewing golden liquid, but somehow he defied gravity and sucked the beer up into his stomach, then repeated the act with the other schooner. Then he unwrapped his legs and dropped his feet to the floor. His partner snatched up the money from the table, gave half to Sluice, thanked Henry and McManus for the beer, and left for another bar.

"I can't believe what I just saw," McManus said. "That was beyond physics. Amazing!" He sounded happier than if he'd won the bet.

"It was just a hustle," Henry said, pissed off that he'd let himself get conned. "A good one, but a hustle. Now I'm about broke. Let's go back to the boat."

"Man, that was fantastic!"

Each hand on the *Carlotta* had ordered a case of duty-free liquor before the season started. Dave Lavernette also stocked a pallet of beer in the hold. The usual procedure for Henry and McManus on their off time was to drink on board until they could feel it, then go into town, where the drinks were expensive. Henry was trying to work up a stake to finance his first record, so he was always the last to leave the boat and the first to return.

That night he and McManus wandered back along the waterfront. The tides in Ketchikan can run up to twenty-five feet. It was high tide when most of the fleet went to town after the opening, and the boats were level with the dock, but that night at low tide, all that was visible of the boats were the power blocks at the top of the masts. As they neared their boat, they saw several groups of fishermen milling around one of the docks, talking in hushed, mumbled tones. Occasionally, one peered over the edge of the dock. Henry stopped at the first group and asked what was going on.

"Oh, the tide fucked somebody from the *Rembrandt*."

Henry cautiously looked down at the deck of the *Rembrandt*, far below, where a body was half covered with an orange rain slicker, two legs jutting out next to a shoe that had somehow come off in the fall. Blood was splattered everywhere in pools and polka dots. Henry felt his stomach turn. He gagged and looked away.

"It looks like his head hit the power winch," someone said.

"That's the first one this year, isn't it?" somebody asked, and several men grunted in agreement. Once every few years, a fisherman would come back from drinking and step right off the dock without thinking, or would slip and fall from the slimy metal rungs down to his boat's deck. Some died; most only ended their season early.

An ambulance rolled up slowly, no lights or siren, to take the body away. McManus and Henry walked farther down to the *Carlotta* and carefully descended to the deck. Henry's hands shook as he climbed down, and he scraped his chest and the side of his face against the wet metal rungs. As soon as his feet were firmly on the deck, he vomited over the rail.

McManus got a bottle from the forecastle while Henry sat down at the galley table and shuffled a deck of cards. He lit a cigarette and tried not to think of the body under the slicker or the blood on the deck, but he couldn't help picturing the dead fisherman as a happy drunk, laughing on his way back to the boat after a night of fun, thinking about getting drunk again the next day, and then, in the space of a second, one miscalculation and his skull shatters like a fish bowl. McManus and Henry spent the rest of the night listening to the radio and playing cards. It was just something to do while they drank themselves home.

At the Polish Club, Henry banked the five ball into the side pocket and wondered why he'd suddenly remembered that night in Alaska. He shivered involuntarily.

"You okay, Henry?" Nappy Baudette asked.

"Yeah, I'm okay. I just felt a little strange for a second." He leaned over the table and lined up his next shot.

THE FIVE of them were in the living room when the doorbell rang. Caroline's mother jumped up and said, "Father Heire's here!"

"Father Heire, here? Tonight? What a surprise!" Stephen said softly out of the side of his mouth, making Caroline smile. At seventeen, he was her baby brother and her favorite. He was small-boned, like Caroline, and only two inches taller. His hair was as straight and dark as hers, though he brushed it back, mostly with his fingers, and didn't wash it very often. He was a great talker, and she loved to listen to him talk about anything—baseball, dairy farming, literature, film, politics, skiing—you name it. Talking was like a sport to him, a competition that got his juices flowing. Though they'd never discussed it, she knew he would never follow their father and brother into the mill. He was an honors student at Edson High and would graduate that June.

Caroline's mother opened the front door. When Father Heire stepped inside, everyone stood and her father strode forward with his hand extended. "Paul," he said. They'd known each other since high school, and Caroline's father took an odd pleasure at being allowed to address a priest by his first name. They shook hands, then the priest unwrapped his scarf, unbuttoned his coat, and handed them to Caroline's mother.

Her father turned to her, standing in front of the couch, and said, "Caroline, fix Father Heire a drink," which meant: Fix both of us strong ones, Scotch on the rocks for the priest and a Seagram's and 7-Up for me. "Come in, come in, Paul. Have a seat. How is it outside?"

"It's downright winter out there," Father Heire said, taking his usual seat in the wing chair by the wood stove. He was six and a half feet tall, the tallest boy ever to graduate from Edson High, and was still as awkward as a teenager who'd grown six inches in one year. "So much for autumn, eh?"

Caroline's father snapped his fingers. "Gone, just like that."

Caroline returned with the drinks and a ginger ale for her mother, who started to get up. But Caroline waved her back down and told her she'd take care of dinner.

In the kitchen, she drained and mashed the potatoes, then drained the string beans. She felt cool beads of perspiration form on her temples. She opened one of the windows a crack to let in some cold air.

"You need any help, Car?" Stephen said, startling her.

"Oh, Stephen! No, thanks." She reached for the serving bowls. Then, thinking he might want an excuse to stay, she said, "Well, you could throw the roast on the serving plate."

"Sure." He opened the oven door.

"So how's school?"

"It's okay. I'm acing everything, which is what I need to do for college. But I can't wait to get out."

"I'll bet. Are you dating anybody?"

"I go out," he said, "but nobody special."

"I don't think there *is* anybody special at that school."

"Try the whole town." He pulled out the roast pan and set it on the white ceramic counter next to the stove. "Okay, Car, tell me something."

"What?"

"Did you go to Mass yesterday?" He carefully lifted the roast from the pan to the serving plate.

"Of course," she said. "Didn't you?"

"I haven't been to Mass in two months."

"Stephen!" she said. "You're the one who's read the whole Bible from cover to cover. You even wanted to be a priest when you were a kid." She started to laugh. "What's going on?"

He shrugged and looked away. "I don't know. It makes me uncomfortable. I just don't like it anymore."

Caroline had never thought of liking or not liking church. It really didn't matter whether you did or didn't. You just went. To miss Mass was a sin.

Stephen looked back at her. "I'm sure Father Heire has noticed, and I bet he says something about it tonight."

"So what are you going to do?"

"Lie my ass off. Tell me what his sermon was about yesterday."

She had to think for a while before it came back to her. "He talked about how it was wrong for women to want to become priests. He said Christ chose twelve men to preach the gospel, and those men were the first priests. Something about how Christ chose men for a reason."

"And what was that reason?" Stephen said.

Caroline thought again. "You know, I'm sorry but I can't remember. I just remember he said there was one. Maybe he didn't say what it was."

"So that was the whole sermon?"

"Pretty much. He did go on at the end about how women shouldn't feel bad about not being priests, because Christ loves them just as much and it's just that they were assigned a different role to complete God's plan."

"Oh, separate but equal," Stephen said. "Some pigs are more equal than others. Wonderful. I'm glad I missed that bullshit."

"Stephen," Caroline said, wagging a finger playfully in front of his nose. "Don't cause trouble tonight."

"I never throw the first punch," he said. "Come on, let's put the food out."

Once everything was on the table, Caroline called them all to dinner.

"Ah, I thought I smelled a roast," Father Heire said, as if he were surprised. "Marjorie, I swear you make the best roast in the world."

Caroline's mother smiled and her cheeks turned pink. She sat down first, then everyone followed.

"Stephen," Father Heire said, "will you do us the honor of leading us in grace?"

At these monthly dinners, Caroline's father abdicated his authority. He still sat at the head of the table, but Father Heire was in control.

Stephen glanced at his sister, beside him. She looked down at her plate. He said grace.

The serving dishes were passed around, and they all filled their plates. Between big mouthfuls of meat and mashed potatoes, Father Heire talked sports with the men and then discussed recent news and town gossip with everyone, especially the Louis Martineau incident from the day before.

"He'll learn from his mistake," Father Heire said. "It's just snowplows, not the end of the world."

"Yeah, he'll learn never to get drunk watching the Patriots lose another goddamn game in overtime," Harold said, laughing alone. When no one said anything, he became very concerned with the food on his plate, then added, "They're from New England. They're just not that good."

Stephen had begun to feel a little more relaxed, when Father Heire turned to him and asked his opinion of Sunday's sermon.

"I think your logic is faulty, Father," Stephen immediately replied, looking directly into the priest's eyes.

Caroline froze with her fork halfway to her open mouth, amazed at her brother's composure.

"Stephen, apologize to Father Heire," his father said.

"No, that's all right, Harry," the priest said. "I'd like

to hear Stephen explain how the Lord's way is faulty."

"I said 'logic,' Father, not 'way'—and it's the Church's logic I'm talking about, not Christ's. They're not necessarily the same thing." Stephen placed his knife and fork neatly side by side on his plate and faced the priest.

Caroline felt her back straighten.

Father Heire drew his hand down across his cheeks hard enough to pull the skin away from his eyeballs, revealing watery red crescents beneath them. "Christ chose twelve men to be the first priests. The Church didn't make that decision. The Lord did."

Stephen wiped his mouth with his napkin. "I don't recall Christ ever saying only men can be priests. I think the Church kind of decided that itself, the way it chose to teach only four of the gospels."

"As opposed to?"

"The Gnostic gospels, Father."

"Those gospels, Stephen, were discredited years ago."

"By whom?"

"By the Church," Father Heire said. "Stephen, Christ expressed his desire by example. He taught us so much by parable and example. And Jesus chose twelve *men*." His voice was low and had the stale, suffocating calm of a late-summer afternoon just before a tornado. His fork clinked as he pushed a piece of roast beef around his plate.

"Whatever you say, Father," Stephen said flatly, as if conceding the argument out of sheer boredom. To win the argument wasn't necessary; he had only to convince the priest he'd been to Mass.

"*Men,*" the priest repeated, as if he wasn't about to let the discussion end.

"Great dinner, Mom," Stephen said brightly, then glanced at his watch. "I hate to leave early, but I've really got to get to the library tonight. Car, do you want me to walk you home?"

"Thanks, Stephen," Caroline said. "But I'll stay and help Mom clean up."

"No, dear," her mother said. "It's dark and icy outside. Cars will be skidding and sliding everywhere. Since you're walking, I think maybe you should go with Stephen. I'll take care of the dishes."

Caroline felt relieved; she wanted to go home.

Then her father said, "I can drive her home after the dishes, Marjorie."

"No; you've had a couple drinks and you'll probably have one more. She should go with Stephen."

Harold said, "I've had a couple myself too."

"All set?" Stephen asked.

She nodded and pushed her chair back. "Great dinner, Mom. Nice to see you again, Father."

"And nice to see you, Caroline."

"Come on, let's go," Stephen said, getting their coats while Caroline kissed her parents goodbye.

Once they reached the end of the driveway, Stephen stopped to light a cigarette.

"Stephen!"

He cupped the cigarette in his hand and took a drag. "Damn. It's cold out here, isn't it?"

"When did you start smoking?"

"I don't know. Who cares?" He started walking, sliding his feet along the sidewalk.

"I do," she said. "Your big sister's dying for a smoke."

"You?"

"Shh. Nobody knows. Just shut up and give me a cigarette."

He took a pack of Marlboros from the deep pocket of his winter coat. He gave her one, then handed her his cigarette to light hers in the wind. She smoked it with her gloves on as they shuffled carefully along the sidewalk toward the hotel.

"I've decided not to go to UNH," Stephen announced. "With my grades, I can graduate early from high school."

She said nothing at first, waiting for him to explain. She just let the wind sting her eyes and kept on walking, smoking her cigarette. "Where would you go?"

"I don't know, but at least it'll be a long ways from Edson. I can tell you that."

"But why?"

"I don't know," he said. "I just have to get away." He was staring straight ahead as he walked, and it scared her. He was only seventeen, and Boston was as far as he'd ever been from home. As far as *she'd* ever been. Stephen was logical and methodical, and he must have thought about this a long time before he told her. But it surprised and upset her that he didn't have a plan.

"Is it living at home?" she asked.

"I really don't know, Car. It's like all of a sudden I can't get comfortable. Don't ask me why. I'm just antsy all the time. I've got to get out of here."

"Is Dad pushing you to work at the mill?"

"No, he knows that's not for me. I don't know what I'm going to do or where I'm going to go."

"Do Mom and Dad know you're leaving?"

"No," he said. "And until I figure this out I'll just keep everything business as usual. But I know I'm leaving, and that's what keeps me going. I feel like I've already left."

As they walked along in silence, Caroline tried to imagine life in Edson without her brother around. A pickup truck with three orange lights over the cab came toward them down the icy street. Recognizing the truck, she hid her cigarette behind her back. But Stephen kept his Marlboro in his mouth, and Caroline saw that he didn't care who saw him smoking anymore. Royal Porter, who was driving the truck, lived three houses away from her parents. Word would get passed around. Caught in the headlights, Stephen took a big drag and smiled as the pickup passed.

When they stopped in front of the residence hotel, Stephen offered her more cigarettes, and she confessed she had plenty in her room. The wind blurred her vision and blew cold through her coat. She hugged her brother a long time, then said goodbye.

HENRY SAW Pope walk into the Polish Club with Beverly Wall, one of the white-beret-and-scarf women who sang at the Millhouse every Sunday. But her silver-blue eyes could stop time, so Pope ignored her affectations. Henry knew she was underage, but she looked old enough to drink and carried herself with a confidence that fooled most bartenders. Larry had once described her as "upwardly nubile." Pope saw Henry and nodded, then ordered two beers at the bar.

Henry had been sitting by himself, nursing what he thought would be his last beer before he went home to bed. He'd been sleeping a lot since returning from Alaska, as much as ten hours a day except for the hunt up at Aaron's cabin. But he was still tired, as if working on the boat had taken something out of him that he couldn't replenish. Watching Pope pay for the beers and lead Beverly Wall in his direction, he wanted to finish his beer quickly and leave. But he was too slow to react, and the moment passed. They had trapped him, and he resented it.

"Mr. Henry," Pope said, taking a seat.

"Mr. Pope. Beverly."

She pulled her chair close to Pope and ignored Henry. He remembered her from when she was a little girl, but if she remembered him, she never let on. Henry preferred it that way. She was so easy to read that he found everything about her, except her eyes, as useless and boring as a paper napkin. The few times Henry had heard her say anything, it was always about the business and not at all about the music. Soon after, Henry noticed that Pope would listen quietly to such conversations, absorbing what everyone said but adding nothing of his own. By now he probably knew more about it than the rest of them. Maybe it was a generational difference. When Henry was younger, he and his friends would talk for hours about songs, chord progressions, solos, vocals, arrangements, and harmonies—hardly ever about percentages, advances, royalties, and contracts, not until it became absolutely necessary. They knew the business side was important and made a point of understanding it in self-defense, but it wasn't something you brought up over a beer. And it took time away from the actual writing and playing of music, which was what they did and who they were.

Henry felt himself growing angry as he sat with the two of them in the Polish Club. It was like undirected drunken anger, but he wasn't even drunk. He looked at Beverly Wall, sitting across the table with her beret and her scarf, and suddenly wanted to say, "You know, kid, your mother has the same eyes. When you were just a little girl at home with your baby-sitter and your mother bartended at the Millhouse, I used to help her put up the chairs at night. The reason she came home late so often was because after everyone had left, I used to fuck her doggy style right up on the stage. I used to make your mother bark like a harbor seal." The thought came out of nowhere, as if it belonged to someone else. Though it was all true, it startled him, and he laughed to himself.

"Mr. Henry?" Pope said.

"Right," Henry said, reeling himself in. But he wanted to say it out loud, wanted to tell Beverly Wall his little story. Though he could hear Pope talking, he didn't feel like listening. He finished his beer quickly and said good night.

RACHEL WAS still out, but Caroline's room was warm and she didn't want it to get cold while she had a cigarette. So she went back downstairs, along the side of the building, and lit up. She'd left her gloves in the apartment, and her hands were freezing.

She heard his footsteps first, softly crunching up the driveway, plodding, then saw him as he moved into the light and crossed the parking lot. It was Henry. She stayed in the darkness and hid the red tip of her cigarette behind her back, but he sensed something and peered into the darkness. He thought he recognized her red parka. "Caroline?"

"Henry?"

"What are you doing out here?"

"I don't know." She dropped her cigarette behind her as she walked toward him, but she saw his eyes follow it into the snow. "Just getting some air."

"Your fingers must be cold."

"My fingers? What do you mean?"

"Well, when your fingers get very cold, it's hard to hold a cigarette unless you really squeeze it."

"I wasn't smoking," she said, knowing she'd been caught.

"Were you not smoking menthols or regulars?"

She paused for a second, then smiled and said, "I wasn't smoking Marlboro Lights."

"Here," Henry said, offering her a Merit. "Try one of mine."

"No, thanks."

"It's freezing out here, Caroline. Let's go inside."

"I don't smoke in our apartment," she said. "Rachel won't allow it and word might get back to my folks and I don't want them to know."

"We can smoke in my place. My parents don't care. Come on."

"All right."

They climbed up the stairs to Henry's apartment. She took off her parka and sat down on the bed. He poured her a glass of wine while she lit her cigarette. She noticed the blinking red light on his phone machine and told him he had a message. He poured a small shot of bourbon and tapped the replay button without thinking. It was Tyler Beckett.

"Hey, Corvine," she said. "Sorry I missed you today. Please call tomorrow. It's important. I'm not leaving the apartment until I hear from you, and I'm supposed to do Letterman on Thursday. So call!"

"Oh, my God!" Caroline said, covering her open mouth with her free hand. "Is that really Tyler Beckett?"

"Yeah." he said, rewinding the machine and sitting in a chair across from her.

"You *know* Tyler Beckett?"

"Yeah." He reached for a cigarette. "She's an old friend."

"But why didn't you say something about it before?"

"It never came up. I didn't see any reason to."

"How did you meet?"

"I think we met at Folk City, one of the clubs in

the Village, probably on some hoot night. I thought she stood kind of funny onstage and told her so. I mean funny in a good way, an interesting way."

"Did you ever go out with her?"

"No, not really," he said. "We used to spend a lot of time together when I was in the city, hanging out and playing music and things like that, but not like a date."

"That's incredible."

"It's really not that big a deal. We were just scuffling along, trying to make the rent and write some music. The folk scene had pretty much dried up by then. Tyler and I hung out together because nobody else would have anything to do with us—except for the other folkies, and most of them were a little weird."

"But she's so famous now," Caroline said. "Isn't that strange for you?"

"To be honest, I just feel happy for her. She's worked her tail off. She's earned it."

"Don't you feel just a little jealous?"

"It's like this," he said, finishing his bourbon and pouring another. "You and Rachel, maybe you're not as close as Tyler and I are, but whatever. Let's say you and Rachel are both working in restaurants, but then you get married and drop out. Ten years later you find out Rachel's the top chef in Boston and newspapers are writing about her and you see her on the local news, and you're married with three bratty kids and never even go out to eat. You'd still be happy for her, wouldn't you? It's something like that. I'm not in the music business anymore, so none of this really matters to me. I'm just happy for Tyler. You want some more wine?"

"No, thanks." She put out her cigarette and lit another. When Henry didn't move toward the phone, she asked, "Aren't you going to call her back? It's still early. Oh, maybe I should leave?"

"No," he said. "I'll call her when I wake up tomorrow. It's no big deal. Right now I feel like getting a little drunk. Come on, let me get you another glass of wine." He took her glass from the nightstand.

"You sure it's okay? I can go."

"No," he said. "I'd like you to stay."

"All right, but only half a glass. I'm still hung over from last night."

Henry hadn't really had any company before in that apartment. Larry and Pope would drop by, but it was always just to pick Henry up and go somewhere else—the Polish Club or some other bar, chess at Larry's. As he poured Caroline's wine he realized how much he liked having her there. He hadn't been alone with a woman to drink or talk or even laugh with since he'd left Laconia in the spring. He hadn't wanted it to be like that, but he hadn't done anything to change it either. He was drunk the two times he'd asked Rachel out, hoping to get laid, and the next morning was relieved she had turned him down. He brought Caroline her glass and sat back down.

"I really meant it when I said I loved your record, Henry. I always thought 'River Beyond the Bridge' was Pope's song."

"Well, that's what he'd like people to think."

"Doesn't that bother you?"

"Yeah, sometimes, but he never claims he wrote it. It's kind of a gray area, and I can't complain, not without looking like an—well, without looking bad."

"But he sounds so much like your record," she said.

Henry didn't want to talk about Pope Johnson, but he wanted to talk. He needed the company. He just didn't feel like explaining it all again. He lit another cigarette and looked at Caroline in the lamplight. She'd taken her shoes off and was leaning back on the bed, holding her drink in one hand and a cigarette in the other.

"You guys are friends, right?" she said.

"Friends? No. We're friendly, but we're not friends. I used to date his sister years ago. That's how we met, when he was just a kid. Don't get me wrong. He's good company and fun to hang out with, but he's an ambitious boy. He's really not anybody's friend."

"I think you might be right," she said cautiously. She still wondered why Pope paid so much attention to her, when other girls could do more things for him—bring him sandwiches at the gas station, drive him to gigs so he could drink without worrying about getting back after the show, do his laundry when he was too busy writing—all while she was waiting tables most nights at the Pilot Inn. But she liked holding him and making love, and always looked forward to seeing him. He made her feel like she was something more than just a girl from Edson.

"I know you go out with him and all that," Henry said. "But that's the way I see it."

"No," she said, sitting back up on the bed and crossing

her legs. "I don't disagree with you. Even though he is that way, he's fun to be with." She wanted him to be more than just fun to be with, but she knew Henry was right. Something had changed in the way she saw Pope after she heard Henry's record, even though she didn't want it to and tried not to think about it. It was as if some mystery had been removed that she hadn't known was there.

"Do you still write songs, Henry?"

"No."

"Why not?"

"I don't, that's all. I don't play anymore. God, I probably haven't even changed the strings on my guitar in years."

"Is that bad?"

"I'd probably need a tetanus shot if I played on those strings."

"But how could you stop?" she said.

He wanted to tell her that it wasn't entirely voluntary, at least not the performing part. He tried to explain as briefly as possible. He'd made two records on a tiny label called Crossroad, but apart from a few reviews, he couldn't seem to get anyone to notice, and sales were dismal. Still, he had his record company's support. As a folk music label, they were used to music outside the commercial mainstream. Henry's records didn't cost much to produce, and both of them eventually ended up in the black. The company encouraged Henry to write well rather than try to write hits. Henry took two years to write the songs for the third album, meticulously working and reworking each line. He recorded them quickly, with only an acoustic bass and an occasional harmonica or second guitar to augment his acoustic guitar and vocal—knowing the sparse arrangements would emphasize his lyrics and melodies. His lawyer told him it could be the breakthrough album they'd been working for.

Henry was in the studio, finishing up the final mix, when his lawyer called to tell him that Seneca—the major label that Tyler would sign with years later—had just bought Crossroad and was taking over his contract.

"So what does that mean?" Henry asked.

"It means you've finally got major-label muscle and money behind you," his lawyer said, excitedly.

It wasn't long before they learned that Seneca wouldn't release the new album as it was. They loved what he'd done, they said, but didn't know what to do with it or how to market it. The sound was too sparse for the current market. If he would cooperate, they were prepared to go all the way with a sizable promotional budget, videos, tour support, and the implied payola—but they needed full band arrangements, heavy on the drums. Henry refused.

"You can't refuse," his lawyer told him. "They bought your contract. They own you for five years. If you don't play ball they can keep you from recording until your contract expires, and your career can't take that. It's already been two and a half years since your last album. At your level you've got to constantly put new product out there to expand your market. You know the economics of it all."

"I think the whole thing's pretty fucking insulting, don't you?" Henry said. There was sadness in his voice, but no anger. He did understand the economics.

"Yeah, it is. Welcome to the music business. So what do you want me to tell them?"

"I don't know. I don't see how I can change the record without ruining it," Henry said.

"And they don't see how they can sell it without changing it."

"When do you have to know?"

"Soon," his lawyer said. "Like tomorrow morning."

"Any chance they'd sell the master back to me?"

"No, you don't want to do that."

"What about the songs?"

"They own the versions you recorded, and you can't record them for anybody else for five years."

"Okay, I'll call you in the morning."

That night he talked it over with his wife, and to his surprise she told him she'd support any decision he made. In the morning he called his lawyer and told him he couldn't change the record.

"I hope you've got a day job lined up," the lawyer said.

"Fuck 'em through the heart," Henry said and hung up. He knew it was false bravado, but in the tone he'd used, it wasn't even bravado. It sounded more like somebody ordering dessert.

At first things remained the same, but without a new album out, the press had no reason to write about him as he toured the country. Radio airplay, which was mostly on college, public, and community stations, began to dwindle because of no new songs. His visibility dropped, and no club in a new market would take a chance on him. His kind of grassroots music required constant touring, physically being in front of people, performing live, winning over new fans, selling albums at the shows. He was left with a finite number of places to work, and one by one they began drying up or going out of business. Henry tried to wait out his contract, but after three years he started feeling strangled, dirty, and tired as he ground out the same songs in the same places night after night. The same budget motels, the same fast food, the same dull faces that had heard all the jokes before. He'd walk through his shows, daydreaming of being somewhere else. He'd drink before shows, show up late, and forget lyrics. He never got enough sleep.

Finally his father-in-law offered him a job with his auto parts business in Laconia, and Henry accepted. He hadn't put out a record in five and a half years and still had two more years to go on his contract. Henry's plan was to work at the auto parts store until his contract expired—to just take a break from the music business—but when that day arrived he couldn't bring himself to go back out on the road. Though he could now legally re-record the songs on the third album for another company, he no longer had the desire or the drive. The need to write and perform had slipped away unnoticed while he was counting mufflers. He liked waking up in his own bed every morning with his wife, and found comfort in the familiar patterns of life with a day job. If it wasn't a thrilling existence, at least nothing hurt. Too much time had gone by, he told himself, to start over in music. No one knew who he was anymore; no one would hire him. He stayed at the auto parts store until his marriage broke up.

When Henry finished his story, Caroline was sitting on the edge of the bed, her feet pressed together on the floor, the wineglass empty in her lap. She knew it was her turn to say something, but she didn't know what to say.

Henry filled in for her. "So that's it, the path of least resistance, I guess." He got up to pour himself another drink—he could feel the bourbon now—and on his way he took her glass and filled it also.

"Do you ever miss it, Henry?" she said. "The music?"

"Sometimes," he said. "Sometimes I think about picking up a new set of strings, but I never do. Or hearing somebody play can make me want to start again, just playing by myself." He laughed out loud. "And sometimes when I hear somebody play well—I mean *really* well—I just want to cut my fingers off." He laughed again, this time softly, as if at a private joke. He handed her her glass and slumped back down. "So what about you?"

"What?"

"Did you ever want to pick up a guitar and get in front of a bunch of drunks and sing them your latest tune?" He didn't hear the bitterness in his voice, but she did.

"No, no, not me. I don't have any talent. No way I could get up there and do what you guys do." She took a sip of wine and lit another cigarette. "One more and I've got to go. It's really getting late. I wonder if Rachel's back."

"I haven't heard her come in."

"No; I imagine she'll be a little late tonight," Caroline said. "She had a date with Lionel Tanner."

"Lionel Tanner?" he said, surprised. He scratched the

inside of his thigh and reached for another cigarette. "Well, that's certainly a step up from her usual assortment of single-cellers, at least financially."

"He picked her up in a limo," she told him.

"That's one way to make an impression."

WHAT HE DREAMED that night had actually happened the past season in Beaufort, before the trip to Ketchikan. The skipper and crew had gone back to their homes after working on the boat all day, laying in supplies and, mostly, painting. That left only Henry and McManus, who lived on the boat. As usual after work was done, they climbed up to the flying bridge to catch a faint breeze and drink a few beers before walking into town for dinner, eight-ball, and drinking. That night before they left, McManus said, "Man, I'm beat. No way I'm walking all the way into town. Let's take the skiff."

Henry sat in the skipper's chair, his feet propped up in the spokes of the wheel. He finished his beer and opened another while he thought about it. He'd already parked his Chevy for the season at his skipper's house in Mount Vernon. Even though some skippers did allow their crews to use the skiffs, Dave Lavernette didn't like anybody using anything unless it had to do with work. Henry knew, though, that either of them could handle the skiff well enough to get them into town and back, and it was a long walk. Besides, Dave had never actually said they *couldn't* take it. "Yeah," he finally said. "Why not? Let's just finish these beers, and then we'll go."

"Sounds good." McManus stared out at the row of purse seiners on their starboard side, all in various states of readiness. Most of the crews had gone home for the day. With one hand, he shielded his eyes from the sun, then he pulled his camera from his pants pocket with the other. Turning his back to the sun, he took a picture of the boats lined up on the port side of the *Carlotta*. "This is the last time I'll be doing all this shit."

"Well, what did you expect? You just passed the bar, for Christsake. You're a fucking lawyer now," Henry said. "You're even getting married this winter, right? I can't believe you came back up here one more time." He lifted his hat off his head and ran his fingers through his hair.

"Yeah, I know. It's just weird."

"Yeah, it is. You could be sitting in some air-conditioned office, making more money than God. Come on, let's drink up. I'm hungry."

"I just wanted to put in one more season," McManus said. After the summer, he was going to join the family law practice in Austin.

"Yeah, one more Thanksgiving dinner at the card table before you have to join the grown-ups."

"Maybe. What the fuck. Who cares?"

They finished their beers, then climbed down into the skiff. McManus started it up and sat in the stern. His cheeks were a splotch of reds and purples above his beard. No one shaved anymore. A beard offered some protection from the jellyfish. Even Henry had started a beard, though it was sparse and McManus told him it made him look like a cross between a Dutch painter and a junked-out Mexican bandit. Henry cast off, and McManus grinned broadly as he eased out into the slough. Henry thought this was much better than walking. He knew that afterward he'd get very drunk.

When they reached town, McManus brought the skiff up behind the restaurant. Henry secured the bow, then climbed onto the dock. McManus fed him the stern line, and Henry fixed it to a cleat. On the patio above them, tourists watched and made comments Henry couldn't make out. It was like being onstage again, and he didn't like it. Henry and McManus walked up the steps and into the bar. A cover band they'd already seen several times was setting up. The first time he'd heard them, Henry shook his head and told McManus they made a good argument for euthanasia.

They each ate a large steak and had several drinks. After dinner they shot pool for drinks against locals and other deckhands waiting for the season to start. At midnight they walked unsteadily out the back door and had to hold on to the railing on the steps down to the dock. McManus dropped heavily into the skiff and started the engine as Henry cast off both lines.

"Goddamn, it's dark out!" McManus shouted over the idling engine.

"New moon!" Henry hollered back.

They started for the *Carlotta*. McManus handled the skiff carefully, but less than halfway back to their boat, in the middle of the slough, the engine died.

"Oh, fuck!" McManus said.

Sitting in the bow, Henry could barely make him out in the darkness.

McManus got the engine to turn over, but it sputtered out immediately. "I think we're out of gas."

Henry lit a cigarette. For a second he saw McManus standing over the engine, then he disappeared with the flame.

In the gentle breeze, Henry leaned back against a coil of line in the bow and shut his eyes. He couldn't imagine being more comfortable and considered sleeping in the skiff—then realized they might have to. He had no idea where they would drift and didn't care. He wondered if the booze was making him think that way, or if he really just didn't care about anything anymore. Either way, he decided, was fine with him. He dropped his cigarette into the slough and tried to sleep.

"Man, we're drifting," McManus finally said.

They drifted for twenty minutes before they heard another vessel puttering toward them, coming from the direction of the restaurant—three hands off the *Crescent Moon*, who towed them home to the *Carlotta*. McManus jumped on board and secured the skiff, then climbed down to his bunk in the forecastle. Henry slept in the skiff until the cold and the gulls woke him at dawn.

RACHEL CAME IN late, drunk. She burst into Caroline's room and switched on the light. "You won't believe the night I had!" she shouted. She sat down at the foot of the bed and almost fell over. "Wake up! Wake up!"

"What is it? What?" Caroline said, disoriented. She blinked her eyes, rubbed them, and looked at the alarm clock. It was two-thirty.

"I just had the most amazing night of my life!" There was no clear space between one word and the next, and Caroline could hardly understand her. Rachel just took a deep breath and let the words fly.

"Tell me," Caroline said, sitting up, knowing she had no choice.

"It was amazing!" She put a hand on the bed to steady herself. "First of all, he had a bottle of champagne on ice, waiting in the limo. Isn't that cool? So we drank the champagne on the way down to Boston. And we start to feel it pretty quick and we get a little giggly and feeling pretty good, so we, like, do it in the limo. Can you imagine? Cruising down the highway at seventy miles an hour, having sex in the back of a limo. He told me I'd just joined the one-foot-high club. Isn't that funny? So then we had a huge Italian dinner at this really cute little place in the North End. And he ordered for me in *Italian*! God, it was so romantic!" She stopped to catch her breath. She sniffed the air. "Have you been smoking, Caroline?"

"No. I was over at Henry's for a while."

"Yeah, he smokes like a chimney. It gets all in your clothes, and it reeks." She crinkled her nose as she sniffed. "You must've been over there for a while." She slipped off her high heels.

"We had a couple glasses of wine," Caroline said.

"And?"

"And nothing. We just had a couple glasses of wine."

"You can tell me," Rachel said.

"There's nothing to tell. But did you know Henry's friends with Tyler Beckett?"

"Yeah, and I'm the Queen of Sheba."

"No, he really is!"

"So anyway," Rachel said, "we drive around the Common and the Public Garden for a while, and it was so beautiful with the snow and everything. We stopped and got out for a walk and he held my hand, but it was too cold, so we got back into the limo. And then he asks me to take off my dress. So I do. No one can see in from the outside. Well, I can tell he really likes the merry widow. He poured us a brandy and we just ride around the city, me in my lingerie, sitting on his lap. And then we did it again, just riding around and around. And he's a wonderful lover, the way he touched me and everything. So we just drive around and do it. We went as far as, like, Maine, I think. I couldn't really see!" She started laughing. "And he just told me he absolutely has to see me tomorrow night, so I have to call in sick at the restaurant."

"That *is* amazing," Caroline said, looking at the clock again. Fully awake, she wouldn't be able to get back to sleep.

Rachel bent down to pick up her heels and, still laughing, rolled right over onto the floor, lying on her back. Caroline saw that her G-string was missing.

"TYLER BECKETT'S office. Lizzie speaking."

"It's Henry. Put her on, please."

"Please hold."

Henry took a sip of black coffee and a drag on his cigarette, one of the Merits. The menthols ran through him in the morning like a laxative.

"Henry," Tyler said. "You're getting harder to find than a first edition of the Bible."

"A signed one, anyway. Morning, dear."

"Thanks for calling. How are you?"

"Fine," he said. "You?"

"I'm still a little wiped out, but it's better each day. It's just great to be home."

"Yeah, I'll bet." He took another drag on his cigarette and coughed.

"Still smoking, huh?"

"Yeah."

"Gotta quit, man," she said. "Get on that nicotine patch or something. That's supposed to work."

"Yeah, I think I will." He thought about his past week up at the cabin with the Nicorettes. It hadn't been horrible without smokes. He was still getting the nicotine he needed.

"I mean it."

"I know. I know," he said. "So how was the tour?"

She laughed. "We covered some miles. I saw Beethoven's birthplace and Jimi Hendrix's grave in the same week. Can you imagine that? The routing sucked at first, but then we worked things out. All in all, it was pretty good, just tiring."

"Where's Hendrix buried—Seattle?"

"Just outside. A town called Renton, I think. So have you been writing?"

"No," he said.

"Have you got a day job?"

"No, but I'm going to have to pick up something soon," he said. "The money I made this summer's getting low."

"What are you going to do? Aren't you going to start gigging again now that you're single?"

"I don't think so. I think I might pump gas or something." It sounded stupid as soon as he said it, and he felt embarrassed.

"That's a good career choice—something challenging."

"Yeah, yeah, yeah."

"Good. Now here's the thing," she said. "This is why I called the other day. You know I can't write on the road, right?"

"Right. I'm the same way. Used to be I could only think about the music. No words."

"Exactly. That's all I've been doing for months. But now the label wants another record—pronto—since they don't hear any other singles off the first. And I just don't have the songs, man. That's why I called."

"Tyler," Henry said, sitting up in his chair. "I don't have any songs either. I don't write anymore. What about the ones that didn't make the first album? I mean, you've got a lot of songs."

"Well, there's a reason they didn't make the first cut, Henry."

"Some of those old ones are pretty close. You could tighten them up."

"I might have to. I still perform 'Slight Rebellion off Madison,' " she said, naming the one song they'd written together.

"Really?"

"Yeah, it gets a great response live, so I'll probably use it. I don't know why it didn't make it on the first record."

Because it was a cowrite, Henry thought, and she'd only get half the royalties. Not that he begrudged her. That was the way the business worked, and Henry hadn't used the song on his albums either. For that same reason, he knew she wouldn't cover anything from his third record. She had no stake at all in those songs, and he was happy that she was considering their one song. Tyler recording that could mean a hefty paycheck for him, though not for a year and a half or two. "No kidding?" he said. "That would be great."

"But I really need your help now. I've got all these ideas and verses and things, and I just need help sorting things out. Some fresh input. I need somebody like you to write the middle eights. Man, your bridges were always so perfect! Nobody could see them coming. You'd jump to a minor fourth when everybody expected a major, and then you'd use that as a stepping-stone into another key, and somehow you'd bring it all back to the original key again for the verse."

"Come on, there's a million guys who can do that," he said. "That stuff's pretty basic."

"Yeah, but *you* know what *I* want! I don't want to work with some fucking hack who just thinks about hits."

Henry didn't say anything. She needed hits.

"Are you still there?"

After several seconds he said, "How do you mean?"

She laughed. "I'm under the gun, Henry. I mean it. I've got to produce. It's not like I can sit back and wait for inspiration, not anymore. You know how it is. You take ten or fifteen years writing your first album and maybe a year for your second, except you're touring your ass off and you don't have time to write. You know that. So won't you help me?"

"Tyler, I don't know if I *can* help you. I haven't written anything in so long and haven't even played guitar. I wouldn't want to waste your time."

"Okay, peckerwood, here's the deal," she said. "Just shut up and listen. I know you won't come to New York. So how about if we meet at the Hilton in Danbury? The ultimate neutral location. I'll get us adjoining rooms. I'll cover your room, a per diem, plus five hundred a week. Of course you'll get a fifty percent writer's share of anything we write. Does that sound okay?"

"It sounds fine, but I haven't done any writing in a long time."

"Come on, Henry," she said. "I need your help. Try it for one week."

"If I was sure I could do you some good, I'd say yes right now, but let me think about it for a day or so."

"Okay," she said. "But sweetheart, I've got to know soon."

"Yes, dear."

"I'll call you tomorrow."

"No," he said. "I'm going up north to hunt. I'll call you in a couple days. Okay?"

"Okay. Soon!"

"I miss you."

"Yeah," she said. "I missed you a lot this year. I went to about every fucking town in the free world, and I didn't see your smiling face anywhere."

"That's because I was catching fish up in Alaska," he said. "They're considered brain food, you know?"

"Yeah, and what do you call that way you fish? Catch-and-release or something?"

"Yeah, that's funny. Look, I'll call you."

"Take care of yourself, Henry. And remember, they've got a great heated pool at the Hilton."

"Really?" He'd stayed at that Hilton and didn't remember anything special about the pool. Maybe they'd put in a new one. "I think my favorite's at the Phoenix in San Francisco."

"With the names painted around it. Yeah, that one's great."

They talked a while longer about motels and hotels, restaurants, delis, and bars—the quirky places musicians all seem to know from touring.

After hanging up, Henry sat motionless for a few minutes. He heard Caroline and Rachel stirring in their apartment. He smoked another cigarette and finished his cooling coffee. He reached under the bed and dragged out his guitar case. He unfastened the snaps and flipped it open. The guitar was a 1963 Epiphone Texan, made in Kalamazoo by Gibson, and its sunburst finish shone in the yellow sunlight, slick, like something well oiled. He hadn't played it since McManus had insisted, late one night on the deck of the *Carlotta*. The time before that, he remembered, it had been snowing.

"HEY, COME ON, get up!" Rachel said, shaking Caroline awake and holding out a cup of steaming coffee.

"What's going on?" Caroline asked, stretching and yawning.

"Shopping," Rachel said. "Remember?"

Caroline took the hot mug and tasted it. Cream and sugar, just the way she liked it. "Shopping?"

"Lingerie. Don't you remember? We're going to pick out something before you go to work."

Caroline marveled at how Rachel could be so alert and energetic with so little sleep. "What time is it?"

"Oh, ten-thirty or something. Come on. Let's go." She pulled the covers back.

"Give me half an hour," Caroline said, covering herself again.

"Okay, half an hour. In the car." Rachel left.

Caroline sat up and rubbed her eyes again. She wanted to sleep in. She sipped her coffee. The two of them would take her Civic, she knew, and drive back home after shopping. Then she'd have some time to herself, an hour and a half or maybe two, before she had to leave for work. She could shower then, she thought.

Tuesdays at work were always slow. Rachel wouldn't

be missed much, and they wouldn't bother calling in another waitress. Caroline would get a few more tables that night, a little more money to pay for what she'd foolishly spend at the mall—for what, and for whom, she didn't really know.

HENRY CALLED McManus down in Austin. The secretary put him right through.

"Henry, you old dog! I've been meaning to get those pictures off to you. I'll put them in the mail this week."

"Great," Henry said. "I can't wait to see them."

"Some of them'll really crack you up. So when you comin' to visit, boy?"

"Oh, Jesus, I don't know," Henry said. "I've got to find a job first. I'm almost tapped out."

"Yeah, well, we did get a little bit fucked. That was one short season."

"Hey," Henry said. "I wasn't at the wheel."

"Yeah, but you know that wasn't Darby's fault. Nobody could see a thing that night." Darby, the lead-line man, was at the wheel the night of the *Carlotta*'s head-on collision.

"Yeah, yeah, I know," Henry agreed. "It wasn't anybody's fault. I'm just a little cranky because I've got to find a job a hell of a lot sooner than I'd planned."

"A day job or a singing job?"

"It better be a day job. I haven't played since that night we got drunk in Cordova."

"There's a million places to play down here, if you want to do that again," McManus said. "I don't know what they pay, but I imagine you'd do okay. Nobody here fingerpicks like you do. It's all strummers, remember? And people still talk about your last show at the Cactus Cafe."

"God, do you know how many years ago that was?"

"It wasn't that long," McManus said. "Hey, Austin's a good place."

"I like Austin just fine, but I just don't feel like straying too far from home right now. Something will turn up."

"You should come down for a visit, though," McManus said. "For the food at least. You remember?"

"Yeah, you can't beat Austin for women or food. You can't get decent Mexican food here. Christsake, they'd boil a fucking taco if they could get away with it."

"Speaking of women, are you seeing anybody?"

"Nah. I don't know what's going to happen with Kitty and me."

"Henry," McManus said, "you're divorced."

"Yeah, but—"

"I don't think there is a *but* this time, old pal. It's over for you two. You gotta realize that and move on. You should just go out and find some high-class mud for your low-class turtle. Get it over with."

"I don't know."

"Well, I do. That's my professional advice as your

attorney. Get your Johnson chomped, then plead nolo. So what kind of work are you looking at?"

"Well, I don't want to work the mill, but I may have to."

"Put that divorce bullshit behind you and figure out what you want to do with your life. There's a lot happening down here, besides music. It might be best for you to clear the fuck out of New Hampshire and start somewhere fresh. We've got plenty of room, if you just want to come down and hang out for a while. I'm not saying music *necessarily*. Now it sounds like you're the one who wants another Thanksgiving at the card table."

"Maybe," Henry said, surprised he'd remembered that line. McManus sounded older, more businesslike than the deckhand who stole a skiff to go drinking. Not unfriendly, just older.

"Well, look, give it some thought, will you?"

"Yeah, I will," Henry said.

They talked a few minutes more, then McManus had to take a business call. Henry hung up, made a sandwich, and reheated his coffee. The more he thought about pumping gas, the more he didn't want Pope's leftovers. The job itself was fine and easy. But Pope had it first, and he was going off to play music.

It was too early for the Polish Club, too early for anything. Larry was getting ready to leave for work—no time to pick up their chess game from the day before.

Henry lay on the bed and stared at the ceiling. Then he got up, called Aaron on the mountain, and said he'd be up for supper.

"THIS IS *not* Johnnie Walker, dear. I don't care what it is, but it's *not* Johnnie Walker *black*. Please take this back and get me a real Johnnie Walker." The woman wasn't more than five years older than Caroline.

Caroline picked up the glass, put it on her tray, and carried it back to the bartender. "Jay," she said, handing him the glass. "She said it's not black label."

"What? You saw me pour it, Caroline," he mumbled. "Johnnie fucking Walker, black fucking label."

"I know," she said.

He topped off the same glass with the same bottle, and Caroline served it.

The woman tasted it and said icily, as if dismissing a servant, "Thank you."

People like that used to bother her, but not anymore. The woman had known it was Johnnie Walker black. She just wanted to exercise power over somebody, and this time it happened to be Caroline.

Pope came in early in the evening. He wasn't drunk, but he'd been drinking. He took a stool at the bar and ordered a beer. She couldn't decide what to say about Henry's album and pretended she hadn't heard it.

"Kinda dead in here, isn't it?" he said. His hands were dirty, and he smelled of gasoline.

"More than usual, even for a Tuesday. It was a little busier earlier."

"How was dinner with your folks?"

"Okay."

He looked around the restaurant. "Where's Rachel?"

"She's kind of sick today."

He reached for the ashtray and lit a cigarette. "Hey, y'all wanna go to New York City this weekend?"

"I can't, Pope. You know I work Saturdays. That's the night I make the most money." She thought of his old car and wondered if what he really wanted was just a ride. Her Civic was only a year old.

"You can take a couple nights off," he said. "You never miss work. Come on, it'll be fun. You ever been to New York?"

"No," she said.

"I'm thinking of moving there soon. Maybe real soon."

"Why?"

"Why?" he said, his voice rising sharply. " 'Cause I'm sick of pumping gas. 'Cause this place blows! 'Cause New Hampshire's full of tight-ass, chickenshit little pricks who spend all their time trying to keep you down. Afraid you might be better than they are! Afraid something worth something might come out of this state."

"Shh. People are looking over here."

"Let 'em, the fuckin' woodchucks! They'll still be sitting here forty years from now, with their thumb up their ass."

"Hey, buddy," the bartender said. "Keep it down and watch your mouth."

Pope dragged hard on his cigarette and said nothing.

"I've got to get back to work," Caroline said, slipping

away to the kitchen, where she hid for a few minutes. When she went out to check on one of her tables, Pope was gone.

She watched the door all shift, but he never came back. She knew he'd spend the night with one of the other girls, but for the first time this didn't bother her. She wondered which one he'd call.

THE GUTTED DEER hung from an oak tree beside the cabin. The blood on the snow looked black in the light from the windows. Henry counted the spikes before he knocked on the door. Dick Sparrow waved him in with his beer.

"That yours out there?" Henry asked, setting his guns down and hanging up his coat.

"Sure is."

"It's a good one." He took a beer from the refrigerator and sat down next to Aaron at the wood stove. Aaron looked to be made up of one color; even his hair was the yellowish gray of newsprint left outdoors for weeks. "Just you two guys here?"

"Perry and Davis left this afternoon," Aaron said. "Burt couldn't make it."

"Where you get your deer, Dick?"

"Base of Firespin."

"Any ideas for tomorrow?" Henry asked.

"Shoot 'em 'fore they get away."

"Thanks, Dick."

"I still see them in the orchard at dusk," Aaron said.

"There and the big bend in the tote road where all that fresh cut is," Dick said. "Are you going to take a stand or still-hunt?"

"I haven't decided."

Aaron got up from his chair and opened the wood-stove door. He picked up two maple logs he'd split the year before and tossed them in. He kicked at one with the heel of his work boot, squeezing it in all the way, then shut the door, leaving a half-inch crack open to draw in air. "Saw a black bear yesterday, went about two fifty, maybe three hundred pounds," he said. "A real big one."

"Where?"

"Right there by the garden." He pointed out the big picture window with his thumb. "I think he was the same one I glassed down in the orchard this summer. I could've taken him from here if my Hawken had been loaded. You can shoot him if you want. He'll be back."

Henry thought about it. He wasn't even sure he still wanted a deer, though he loved venison and enjoyed pursuing game. But this trip his heart wasn't in it completely—as if he'd had his chance the week before and didn't deserve another one. Maybe he should go after the bear instead, he thought. Hunting bear with a single-shot muzzle loader didn't leave much room for error.

But at least he was back at the cabin, hunting, doing something, not just lying on his bed, staring at the ceiling and waiting for somebody to get off work.

"Henry," Dick called from the kitchen. "I forget. How do you like your steaks? I never can remember."

"Medium rare," he called back.

"That's how I always liked them," Aaron said. "Enjoy it, you bastard!" he added jokingly. With the medication and treatment, many of the foods he loved had become repugnant to him.

Dick brought a bottle of Jim Beam and two glasses. He handed one to Henry and filled it, then asked Aaron if he wanted more water. When Aaron shook his head, Dick poured himself a bourbon. "To your good luck tomorrow, Henry," he said.

"Yes," Aaron said. "If you get your deer, it'll be the first time in eleven years that *all* the tags were filled, even though it's not black powder season anymore. Are you using the Hawken or the Ruger, Henry?"

"I planned to at least start with the Hawken," Henry said. "It depends on how frustrated or hungry I get."

Dick and Henry drank, while Aaron got up again and opened the wood-stove door so they could watch the flames. Dick and Henry had a second glass and decided they could wait awhile before starting the steaks. Around nine, Aaron got up, and Dick walked him to his bedroom. Dick was fifty-one, ten years younger than Aaron, and they'd been friends ever since Dick had come up from Arkansas, fifteen years earlier, to teach at the university in Durham, where Aaron taught. Dick was on sabbatical this semester and mostly running the hunting camp, taking care of things Aaron couldn't do anymore. Dick came back into the main room with a new bottle of Beam. He sat down where Aaron had been sitting.

"So," he said, cracking the bottle open. "I didn't get a chance to ask you last week, with everybody here and all, but are you legally divorced yet?"

"Yeah, early August." He held out his glass.

"Man, that's a bitch. I remember my divorce was no picnic. Did it come as a surprise, the breakup?"

The bourbon felt good, and Henry didn't care about the divorce right then. "Yeah, it did," he said. "But I should've seen it coming when she started serving me pork tartare for supper."

Dick smiled. "So what are you doing now?"

"Nothing." Since this sounded to Henry like the wrong answer, he tried again. "I might start writing again."

"Really?"

"Yeah. Tyler Beckett wants me to help her with the songs for her next record."

"That singer with those Buddy Holly glasses? You know her?"

"Yeah," Henry said. "She's an old friend." He knew he was saying things he wouldn't if he was sober, but he didn't care.

"Would that pay?"

"It could pay."

"Then what are you waiting for?" Dick said. "These things don't fall into your lap every day."

"Yeah." Henry took a long drink. "It's just that I haven't written anything for years."

"If you went hunting after a ten-year hiatus, you couldn't get yourself a deer?"

"Not without shooting a couple toes off first."

HENRY'S CAR wasn't in the lot behind the hotel. Then Caroline looked up and saw no lights on in her apartment or Henry's. She walked around to the front door and climbed up the stairs. She heard music playing in Larry's apartment. Inside hers, she hung up her coat and opened the refrigerator for a beer. But all she had was vodka and nothing to mix it with except orange juice, and she didn't feel like a screwdriver. Larry always had beer. She crossed the hall and rapped on his door.

"Hey, Caroline," Larry said, holding a paperback book and smiling.

She started to ask for a beer, then stopped and cocked her ear to the music. "That's Henry, isn't it?"

"Right."

"My God, you've got Henry's record and you never said anything about it?"

He shrugged, a little confused. "It's an old record. I haven't listened to any vinyl since I got my CD player, and that was . . . what—two years ago? Before you moved in, anyway."

"What is it around here? Am I the only one who . . ."

She stopped to listen. It wasn't a song she'd heard on the album at Pope's. "You have *both* records?"

"Yeah, sure."

"Okay," she said. "You wait right here." She went back to her apartment and got the blank cassette she'd bought at Martello's, then crossed the hall back to Larry's. "I want you to make me a tape of both records right now. You don't have a choice. I'll pay you back somehow, but please, you have to."

He looked a little bewildered. "Okay. I mean, it's late, but I was going to be up for a while, anyway. You want a beer?"

"Yes." Then she thought and said, "Oh, I'm sorry. Let me get you something stronger from my apartment. Do you like vodka? That's all I've got."

"No, that's all right," he said. "I only drink beer. Come in and get comfortable. This will take a while, but I've got plenty of beer."

Caroline sat down on one end of his couch while he unwrapped the cassette, put it in the deck, and set the recording levels.

"Oh, wait a minute," she said, jumping up. "I forgot something." She ran across the hall for her cigarettes and matches. Back at Larry's, when she sat down on the couch she saw Larry had opened a can of beer for her and poured half of it into a pilsner glass.

"Are you ready?" Larry asked. Then he saw the cigarette in her hand and raised his eyebrows. "Well, this is a surprise."

"No more than finding out you've got both of Henry's records. Even he doesn't have any copies! And did you know he recorded a third record?"

"I knew he didn't have any copies," Larry said, "but I never heard anything about this third record. Did he tell you that?"

"Last night. It was never released. There aren't any copies of that one."

"Yeah," Larry said, thinking. "I didn't know about that." He held up both record jackets. "Which one would you like to hear first?"

"The one I haven't heard. The one that's on. Play that first."

"You know," Larry said, starting the cassette and the turntable, "if it weren't for Henry, there wouldn't be a—"

"Pope Johnson," she said. "I know." She slipped a cigarette between her lips and lit it. "Pope just told me he's moving to New York."

"Really? When?" Larry thought it was strange Caroline was smoking, but didn't say anything. He took his book back to his easy chair and looked over to where she sat on the couch, her beer glass in her lap.

"Soon, I think," she said. Her eyes shut, she rolled her head back and smoked her cigarette as she listened to Henry's weary voice, a faint smile crossing her face.

THE WIND BLEW across the black sky and dared him to come out, but Henry waited for his alarm. The room was cold. He'd gone to bed wearing socks, long johns, an insulated top, and his old, hooded fishing sweatshirt, but he was cold, even under the covers. He knew the rest of his clothes, piled on the floor, would be cold. He saw the black shapes of hemlocks rocking helplessly in the wind that whipped down from the mountain. A gust of wind hammered against the glass, and Henry pictured a crowd, panicked, pressing up against a chain-link fence, trying to get in to safety. He closed his eyes and drifted back to sleep.

At five o'clock, when the alarm went off, Henry killed it quickly so as not to wake Dick or Aaron. He flicked on the little table lamp on the chest of drawers, and the first thing he saw was the Renoir print of a young girl with a sprinkling can. The Picasso, he knew, was on the wall behind him. He always stayed in the same room at the cabin, Aaron's daughter's room. She now taught freshman English at the university. When Henry first moved to Edson, they had lived together. That was how he'd become friends with Aaron in the first place.

Henry dressed and walked quietly to the kitchen to put on the coffee, then opened the wood stove and stirred the embers with the iron poker. He blew on them until they glowed. Taking three small birch logs from the woodbox, he put them in the stove, adding maple and beech on top. Though it wouldn't burn for long, the birch would get a good blaze going and start the other logs.

Once the fire was going strong, he poured himself a cup of coffee and took it to the chair in front of the picture window, where Aaron spent most of the day with his binoculars. It was still pitch black outside, and the wind blowing on the other side of the window told him to stay inside and go back to bed. He finished his coffee, poured another cup, and made a sandwich, which he stuffed into a pocket in his orange hunting coat. He wanted a cigarette but opened a Nicorette instead. It was better than nothing. Finishing his coffee, he put on his coat. He slipped the percussion cap on his Hawken and eased the hammer down to half-cock safety, then buttoned every button on his coat and walked out into the cold. He had to be on his stand before the first hint of daylight.

He'd decided over coffee to hunt the fresh cut at the big bend in the tote road. There he'd be protected from the wind coming down off the mountain and sweeping across the clearing, and downwind from any game. It was a little swampy where the sharp ascent of the mountain began, and Henry had caught fish in the small stream that gurgled nearby, cutting a winding black path through the fresh snow. He took cover behind a hardwood blowdown nearly three feet across and, freezing in the dark, waited for the sun or a deer. He didn't care which came first.

The first deer, a small buck the color of a wet maple, crept along the far edge of the clearing just as it became light enough to shoot. The wind had died down, and everything was cold and still. Henry stiffly got up onto one knee and leaned into the blowdown, resting the rifle on it as he pulled the hammer back to full cock. The click sounded loud enough to cause an avalanche, but the buck didn't seem to hear, and Henry framed him in the iron sights. He was still too far away, two hundred yards, to risk a shot. The Hawken was primitive, and Henry never took shots over a hundred yards. He could easily have taken the deer with his Ruger, just set the crosshairs right behind the shoulder and pulled the trigger, but he liked the feel of the Hawken, liked the eggy smell of black powder and greased linen patches and the soft, heavy feel of round lead balls he'd cast himself. He tracked the deer in his sights, but he came no closer and finally drifted off into the brush.

The hollow was still hidden from the sun, but the sky was turning blue overhead and the temperature had risen noticeably when the second buck appeared—a large buck following three small does boldly, stupidly, across the center of the clearing. The buck's neck was swollen with the rut.

Henry's heart thumped against his rib cage, and his hands shook. He'd never been presented with such good fortune, and he had to fight to keep from laughing. You horny old bastard, Henry thought. You're crazy with the rut. The buck was beautiful, majestic, and dumber than mud. Henry pulled the set trigger and lined up his sights. He'd slipped into another world now, one of instinct and snap decisions. The buck would offer him a pure broadside shot in seconds. There was no other world or time. Henry didn't even hear the bear thrashing through the woods behind him until he stopped and snuffled and roared. Henry spun around as the bear stood up ten feet behind him. He stood up and hollered back, then brought the Hawken up to his shoulder again.

The bear dropped to all fours and held his ground.

They stared at each other. Henry heard the deer running in the clearing behind him, their hooves making a dull, rhythmic sound like a hundred heartbeats. Neither Henry nor the bear moved. Minutes crept by. The Hawken, at ten pounds, gained weight with each minute. The bear's eyes were the same runny yellow as his teeth, and they seemed to be searching for a weak spot in Henry's soul. A cold, gentle breeze wandered down from the mountain into the hollow and brushed past the bear to Henry, who gagged on the smell of decaying meat and death.

The bear was bigger than Aaron had said, easily over three hundred pounds. Henry remembered reading that someone had taken a four-hundred-pound black bear with a Hawken a few years earlier. The bear stared at him, and he stared back. Neither of them wanted to be there. After fifteen minutes, Henry realized he had broken into a sweat and was shaking. The gun had become too heavy to hold any longer, and he had to either put it down or shoot. He had a clear chest shot, but his hands were trembling too much. Instead, without thinking, he stomped his foot as hard as he could and screamed a short, clipped "Hey!" and the bear spun around and hurried off into the woods, kicking up snow and mud and leaves, cutting through a stand of alders that sprang right back up to their original positions.

Henry sat back against the blowdown, then slowly walked up the tote road to the cabin. Before going in, he went through the ashtray in his car and found two cigarette butts.

CAROLINE WOKE UP early, but at least Rachel hadn't awakened her in the middle of the night again. She remembered she'd taped Henry's albums, and that made her get out of bed and throw on her robe. She crept over to Rachel's door and silently turned the knob to make sure the bed was empty. Then she got the cassette and put it on while the water heated for coffee. It was eight o'clock, and she didn't have to be at work until three.

INSIDE THE CABIN, Aaron and Dick were drinking coffee in the main room.

"Didn't hear any shots," Dick said.

"I saw the most beautiful, regal buck crossing the middle of the clearing, with three does ahead of him," Henry said, "when a bear jumped up behind me, for Christsake!"

"Why didn't you shoot him?"

"I don't know," Henry said. He scratched his cheek as he thought about it. "When he came on me I was lining up the biggest damn buck of my life. Maybe I was just thinking deer."

"That's kind of odd," Aaron said. "Black bear aren't

like that. Nine times out of ten they see you first and take off."

"I know," Henry said. "I think we kind of surprised each other."

"What color was he?" Aaron asked.

"Cinnamon."

"So was the one I saw out there," Aaron said. "I'll bet it was the same guy. So what happened?"

"We stared at each other for I don't know how long, maybe half an hour, then I stomped my foot and shouted, and he ran off. God, did he stink!" Then he excused himself, went to his room, and packed his things. When he returned to the main room, he took his Hawken outside and fired at nothing, out toward the mountain. Then he cased it and said goodbye.

"My mind just isn't on hunting right now. I'm heading back to Edson."

Going down the mountain in the snow was trickier than coming up. He rode the brakes and tried to anticipate the curves, but when he hit the flats he started to relax. He stopped at the first general store and bought cigarettes and a six-pack. Back on the road, he kept a beer between his thighs. It wasn't until he was halfway to the interstate that he could think about the bear. It was an accident, a fluke, that they'd met up at all. The wind hid his scent, and the bear had no idea he was there in the hollow. All Henry could think about was the moist yellow eyes, the stench. He should've killed him, he thought.

In Bristol, near the interstate, he stopped in the parking lot of the grocery store and finished another beer. He watched the traffic for a long time, then drove back toward the mountain. It was late morning. He could get up to the cabin and to the clearing by dusk. He didn't know why he was turning around, but nothing was making much sense anymore. He just wanted to see what would happen if he faced that bear a second time. And what else was there to do but go back to his apartment, get drunk, and stare at the ceiling?

RACHEL CAME HOME at two that afternoon. She dropped her purse and coat on the divan and called in sick again at the restaurant.

"Hi," Caroline said. "You okay?"

"God, I haven't slept all night. I've got to get to bed." Rachel looked drawn and thin, as if she hadn't eaten anything in days.

"Good night," Caroline called as she disappeared into her room. Then she took the cassette out of the deck and slipped it into her parka pocket. When she left for work she checked at the desk in the lobby to see if there was any mail.

The desk clerk smelled of whiskey and dirty clothes. "Well," he said, "I'd say your whole wing hit the jackpot." He piled four identical packages on top of each other on the desk. They were from the Tanner Shoe Company, addressed to Larry, Henry, Rachel, and herself.

Caroline stepped back. She hadn't ordered any shoes or boots.

"And Corvine got these two little things," the clerk added. "Both overnight, one from Texas, the other from New York City."

She took everything but Larry's package up to her apartment, set them on the kitchen counter, and walked back down to the lobby. Crazy Betty was sitting in her chair, smoking a cigarette and looking out the window. When she asked for a cigarette, Caroline told her she didn't smoke, as usual, and Crazy Betty was disappointed, as usual.

As she walked to her car, the idea came to her that maybe Lionel Tanner had sent them all something, maybe just to do a nice thing. It certainly wouldn't cost him anything.

NEITHER DICK nor Aaron had seemed surprised when Henry returned that afternoon. It was as if he'd gone into town for supplies.

Henry carried a bucket of garbage toward the same blowdown. Aaron had tried to talk him into taking the Ruger .308, but Henry had insisted on the Hawken. "It'll be a close shot," Henry told him.

He walked down the tote road, crunching the hard, dry snow with every step, following the bootprints of the earlier hunters, himself included, holding his Hawken in one hand and the garbage pail in the other. The rest of the county still enjoyed an early winter sunset, but down in the hollow, hidden in the shadows of the tall evergreens, it was dark. Behind him, through the leafless hardwoods to the east, he could make out the cabin, still catching the sunlight. He poured the garbage around a stump near the edge of the clearing, then set the bucket on top. He rested his back against the blowdown, hidden, listening to the naked branches scraping in the wind. When the wind died down he could hear the stream.

Henry shivered as the sun dropped completely behind the mountain. Inside his wool gloves, his fingers ached from the cold, and he flexed them to get his circulation going. It wasn't that late. The bear, he knew, would make his rounds early in the evening.

After an hour the moon rose, almost a three-quarter moon, and Henry could see the outlines of the trees against the snow. Everything was still. The cold seemed to come up from the ground. He knew it was past legal hunting time, but he stayed. Then he heard the bear at the bottom of the mountain, pushing his paws through the snow, crossing the stream. He'd caught the scent of the garbage. Henry rested the rifle barrel on a fat branch, pulled the hammer to full cock, squeezed the set trigger, and waited. The bear kept coming. Then Henry felt the first irritation in his nostrils, a sneeze beginning to build. The bear rumbled closer, and Henry held his breath. He knew he'd be able to make out its rolling silhouette at any second. He held his nostrils closed with his left hand, but the urge suddenly became too powerful, and he sneezed. He managed to muffle part of it, but the bear stopped instantly, and the mountain fell silent. Then the second sneeze came, loud and full, like an aftershock, and the bear crashed back up the mountain and was gone.

Henry sat up, stunned, thinking it was too bizarre to be disappointing, too capricious to be anything but funny. "I sneezed," he said out loud. "Yes, Henry, you sneezed and scared a bear. Probably would've killed him if you'd farted too." He lit a cigarette and started up the tote road, chuckling. He'd never heard of anything like that happening before. "I sneezed," he said again, not really believing it, thinking of how he'd tell Dick and Aaron over a drink.

Feeling oddly good for the first time in a long while, he wasn't really sure why and didn't care. He just savored the feeling.

DRIVING DOWNTOWN toward the Gulf station, Caroline thought it was too early to be that busy on Main Street, too early for the first shift to let out and the second to come on. Nobody seemed to be going anywhere, in or out of the mill. Traffic was light, and the people crowded the sidewalk as if they were waiting for a parade. Maybe, she thought, there was a power outage or something at the Tanner Company.

HENRY CAME DOWN off the mountain after lunch. He had slept in that morning instead of hunting, resigning himself to a winter of venison handouts, steaks Dick would offer him and dinners here and there with others. He could do worse, he knew.

It was another sunny day, above freezing, and melting snow dropped off tree branches in handfuls. He drove slowly through Bristol, looking for people he knew, enjoying the Thanksgiving decorations in the windows of shops he used to visit before he and Kitty moved out to the farmhouse. He was working on his second record when they lived here. He thought about his ex-wife, and then about Caroline listening to his first record. Kitty had the records and the tape of his unreleased album in Laconia. At the entrance to the interstate, he passed underneath it and stayed on the two-lane toward Laconia. It was a roundabout way back to Edson, but he wanted to hear what he had done years ago and, if anything held up, to play it for Caroline. He didn't want her to know only his first, unsteady work, no matter how much she liked it.

He didn't stop to call in advance, since Kitty worked only mornings on Thursdays at her father's store. When he turned into the dirt road that led to his farmhouse and rounded the final bend, he saw the bright-red Toyota gleaming in the sun against the faded yellow shingles and the white snow. He pulled in behind her truck, walked to the long, screened-in side porch, and knocked on the kitchen door, his heart beating quickly. Suddenly it surprised him how much he wanted to see her again, just to look at her, to hear her voice.

She jumped back and brought her open hand up to her windpipe when she saw him through the window. For a second she looked terrified, then she smiled and reached for the doorknob. "Hi," she said. "This is a surprise. Come on in." Her voice was high and sounded like it belonged to the cartoon of a woman.

Henry smiled at the sound of her voice. "Hi," he said, stepping into the kitchen.

"Give me your jacket," she said. "You want a coffee or a beer or bourbon or something?"

"Sure, why not? I'll have a bourbon." He handed her his coat, sat down at the kitchen counter, and watched her pour him a drink. She had put on weight in the face, he thought, maybe all over. He couldn't tell because she was wearing a baggy pair of bib overalls over a pink sweatshirt that had *Puerto Rico* written on the front. He remembered the sweatshirt from when they were married, but had never known where it came from. He lit a Kool Mild.

She handed him his drink and poured herself a glass of apple juice. "It looks like you've been hunting."

"Yeah."

"Get your deer?"

"No. You're not going to have a drink with me?"

"In a bit. You want to go into the living room?"

"Fine."

She led the way into the living room, where a larger wood stove blazed. It was noticeably cooler in the room between the kitchen and the living room. Most people would have used it as a dining room, but they'd never gotten around to getting the furniture. Henry liked it that not much had changed in the house since he moved out. He noticed the woodbox was low and made a mental note to fill it for her before he left.

"So I was on my way back from Aaron's and thought I'd say hi and see how you're doing. That and pick up a couple things."

"You look good," she said, but he knew she didn't mean it. He looked like somebody who'd been living on bourbon and nicotine for the last six months. "How's Aaron doing?"

"Well, he's sick. He's dying. I don't know."

"I'm sorry. How was Alaska? You look like you got some muscles."

"It was hard," he said, "and short. One of the deck-hands cracked up the boat and nearly sunk us one night. That was the end of the season for us. Besides I'm too old for that shit." The only contact he'd had with her since he'd left for Beaufort was a postcard giving her his Edson address and number. Her only response was to tell him they were now legally divorced.

"I thought you came back early," she said. "Are you working?"

He shook his head and took a drink.

"Did Tyler reach you?"

"Yeah."

They made small talk for a while, caught up on gossip, laughed a little. The talk came easily, and he enjoyed himself. It began to cloud over outside. Finally he explained that he wanted to pick up copies of his records and the tape of his third.

"Of course," she said. "But when did you start listening to your own music? You used to turn the radio off when one of your songs came on."

"I'm just curious to see what they sound like. It's been a long time."

"Are you playing again?"

"No." He looked at his watch. "Look, I really should go."

"I'll get your stuff," she said, slowly getting up. As the coveralls stretched around her, Henry saw she'd put on a lot of weight in her thighs and belly. He didn't know why, but he was glad.

When she was in the den, he got up to see what had been added to the bookshelf. She loved to read more than anyone he'd ever met. As he lit another cigarette, he noticed that all the cigarettes in the ashtray were his. She hadn't smoked at all.

"Here you go," she said, returning with the records and the cassette.

"Did you quit smoking?" he asked.

"Uh, yeah, I finally did." She looked away.

"Well, good for you. I've got to quit myself. Did you get on the patch?"

"Nope," she said. "Cold turkey."

They said an awkward goodbye at the kitchen door, neither of them knowing what to do. He hugged her lightly and waved as he backed his car out.

He was halfway to Edson before he added everything up. He pulled the Chevy into the first convenience store he came to and called her.

"Hi," she said. "You forget something?"

"Yeah, I forgot to ask you two things."

"Shoot."

"One, when is the baby due? And two, is it mine?"

She said nothing for a long time, as if she were calculating figures to give an estimate on something at the auto parts store. "I'm sorry, Henry. I was going to tell you soon. I really was. And when you just showed up today out of nowhere, I just couldn't think of a way. But the baby's due in March, and no, it's not yours."

"I can't believe you didn't say anything."

"I'm sorry."

"Who's the fucking father?" he demanded.

"Mickey."

"Mickey! From the store? Are you fucking crazy? Are you out of your mind?" Mickey was twenty-seven and had aspirations to become a professional wrestler. "He doesn't have the brains of a bivalve! Jesus Christ. How long have you been fucking him?"

"We started seeing each other this summer, after you left."

"Bullshit!"

"Honest, Henry. After you left."

His mind raced back to the last few months of their marriage, trying to find clues that could've tipped him off. "Why?"

"He's good to me."

"I was good to you."

"No you weren't," she said. "Not toward the end."

"What do you mean?"

"You were always drunk and cranky. You never should've refused making those changes on the record. You should've done what they wanted, at least until you sold a lot of records."

"But you agreed with me."

"No, I went along with what you wanted. That's different."

He knew she was right, and couldn't think of anything to say.

"I'm sorry," she said.

"Me too." He suddenly felt completely drained. Mickey would be good for her in some ways, he knew. He could fix anything around the house, would do whatever she told him to, and as long as he worked for her father, would always be an adequate provider. He just couldn't form a simple, complete declarative sentence, and Henry felt his own marriage cheapened. "Are you going to marry him?"

"I don't know," she said.

"You told me you couldn't be married to anyone again, ever."

"Yeah, I know," she said.

LATE THAT AFTERNOON the wind picked up and blew hard across the river. Whitecaps formed. Two Moran tugs bobbed up and down at the dock next to the Pilot Inn as the happy hour crowd, mostly regulars, trickled into the restaurant.

"You're from Edson, aren't you, Caroline?" Eddie asked. He was a travel agent in Portsmouth, and though he tipped well, Caroline didn't like him. He thought tipping gave him license to act more familiar than she wanted.

"All my life," she said.

"Sorry to hear about the mill." He put his hand on her forearm.

"What?" she said, stepping back. "What about it?"

"You don't know?"

"No, what?" She tried to imagine what could have happened—a fire, or a strike?

"It's closed," he said. "Gone. They moved out of town."

"They can't move out of town," she told him, irritated.

"Well, they did."

"My father works there. He says the mill's making lots of money. Everybody needs shoes, you know. And why would they leave?"

"To make *more* money," Eddie said. "I heard they're relocating the whole thing down to Tennessee or Georgia or someplace."

"But why?"

"Who knows? Tax breaks, cheaper labor and heating costs, no union problems."

"But they've always been in Edson."

"Up until last night," he said. "They're gone now." Then he ordered another Stinger.

Caroline set her tray down on the bar and began to dial home. "Not now, Caroline," the bartender said. "We're getting too busy."

"But I've got to call home."

"As soon as it slows down," he said.

"No, you don't understand."

"Later, Caroline."

She hung up, put in Eddie's order, and served him his drink.

THE FIRE was visible miles away as an orange glow low in the night sky, beyond some hills. Henry knew a glow that size meant a monstrous fire, and when he saw the actual flames rising up he hoped it wasn't the hotel—aside from the mill, the only building big enough to cause such an inferno. But as he passed the Blessed Virgin and crossed the town line, the hotel and the mill were intact and he saw the fire was somewhere across town, over by Elm Street.

Henry stopped at Martello's for cigarettes and more beer. He'd done nothing in the last few hours but drive blindly around the back roads, drinking and smoking.

Debbie Martello, behind the counter, was the only person in the store. "Why ain't you over to the fire?" she asked.

"I've been up hunting. What's burning?"

"Them three big Tanner houses," she said slowly, as if it was some sort of achievement.

"Jesus! All three? Do you think it was set?"

"Christsake, I don't guess it was spontaneous combustion!" She laughed.

"I hope none of the Tanners got hurt."

She laughed again. "Don't think so. Not unless they got into a freakin' traffic accident on the way to Tennessee, and that would be just fine with me. A good head-oner, Tanners just flying through the windshield."

"What are you talking about?"

"Christsake!" she said. "The goddamn mill locked its goddamn doors and moved out of town last night! They're moving the whole damn operation down to Tennessee somewheres. Just like that! Didn't let on to nobody, them bastards!"

Henry didn't know what to say, so he paid for his cigarettes and beer and got back into the car. The flames from the three mansions lit the sky and sent a warm wind through the town's streets. It felt like a late-September night, Henry thought, except that snow was melting and dripping everywhere. Henry drove back to the hotel to drop off his car, and decided to have a shot of bourbon before he left to watch the fire.

Upstairs, he was surprised to hear the television coming from Rachel and Caroline's apartment. They both should've been at work. He dropped all his gear off in his apartment, then knocked on their door.

"What the fuck do you want?" Rachel said. Then, before he could answer, she said, "Oh, yeah, you got some mail. Here." She put her beer bottle down and handed him the Tanner Company box and both overnight envelopes. She was wearing a white cotton nightgown with lilacs the size of half-dollars printed all over it.

"What's this?"

"Shoes, boots, what difference does it make?" she said.

"I didn't order anything."

"Nobody did," she said. "Larry sent them from the shipping department."

"What's going on around here?"

"What do you think is going on? Jesus Christ, the mill, like, pulled out of town! Where the fuck have you been?"

"Yeah, yeah, I heard about the mill. What's the big deal to you?" Then he remembered she'd just started dating Lionel Tanner. "Did Lionel clear out with the rest of them?"

"What the fuck do you think?" she said, finishing her beer and getting another from the refrigerator. She didn't offer him one.

Henry pulled the door shut behind him. In his apartment, he tossed the box and the envelopes on the bed unopened, then uncased his guns and stood them up in the homemade rack on the floor. He put the six-pack in the refrigerator. He poured a whiskey and played back his phone messages.

"Henry, it's Tyler," the voice said. "Have you decided yet? I know you can do this. You're the best. Just say yes. Letterman tonight. Call me tonight and tell me what you think of the tape."

Henry didn't know what tape she was talking about, and he didn't want to think about anything.

Another fire engine roared down Main Street, dragging a siren in its wake. He opened his window shade and looked in the direction of the fire. Off to the east, the flames were shooting high into the sky as fast as whips, and he decided to walk over to Elm Street to see for himself. He knew that's where half the town would be. He poured another shot, then zipped up his coat. In the distance he heard another fire engine. He'd finish unpacking and open his mail when he got back.

BUSINESS AT the restaurant slacked off around nine-thirty, and by ten only half a dozen customers were left in the lounge. Caroline had called home an hour earlier, but the line was busy. At ten-fifteen she asked the bartender if she could get off early since it was so slow.

He said it was all right with him, and she drove straight home.

Her mother was alone in the living room, watching television.

"Where is everybody?" she asked.

"At the fire, I imagine," her mother said, as if they couldn't possibly be anyplace else.

"What's burning? You can see the flames for miles!"

"Somebody set fire to the three Tanner houses." Her mother stared at the television as she spoke.

"Oh, my God!" Caroline said, sitting down next to her on the couch. "Was anybody hurt?"

"No. Everybody was already gone."

"So it's true, then. The mill's closed."

Her mother explained the story the way Caroline's father had explained it to her at lunch.

The night before, halfway through the third shift, at three in the morning, the Tanner brothers told the workers to go home, explaining that the machines had to shut down for safety inspections and that everyone would be paid for a full shift. When the last worker had punched out, the Tanners finished packing up their offices, turned off the lights and heat and water, locked all the doors, and began the two-day drive down to Tennessee, where their families had already relocated. A brand-new mill was waiting for them there.

"What's going to happen now?" Caroline asked. "What's Dad going to do—and Harold?"

Her mother pulled her close. "Everything's going to be all right," she said. "Your father's already taken care of everything. He called your uncle Freddy this afternoon and lined up jobs at the Dorr Mill. Uncle Freddy's a foreman now, you know."

"But that's in Newport!" Caroline said. "That's almost in Vermont. You'd have to move."

"We don't have a choice, honey. I'm not happy about it either—I've never lived anywhere else but here in Edson. But your father would never find a job around here, not with everybody else from the mill looking for work too. Right now you've got to take whatever you can get, and the longer you wait, the harder it's going to be. That's just the way it is."

"But what about Stephen?"

"Well, he's only seventeen. He's got to come with us."

"He could stay with me until the school year is out," Caroline said.

"I don't think so, dear. In fact, we think you should come with us too."

Caroline had to change the subject. "And what about the house?"

"Well, we'll try to rent it out, I guess, or maybe sell it. Your father hasn't decided. If it was a different time of year we could rent it to students, though I don't know if I'd want to do that."

"Rachel and I could rent it. We could even find a third roommate for the extra bedroom."

"I don't think so, dear. You'll be with us. I'm sure you can find a perfectly good job waitressing, if that's what you want. Or I imagine your father can find you something at the mill offices. As he said, you're good at that sort of work. You got that from me. That's what I did before I had Harold."

"I'm going to go see the fire," Caroline said, eager to end the conversation.

Her mother got up from the couch and strained to look out the side of one of the front windows. "Better walk, dear. They won't let cars anywheres near."

"Have you been down to the fire?" Caroline asked.

"For a while, early on."

"Well, I'm going down to take a look, then I'm going back to my apartment. Call me if you need anything, Mom."

"We'll be all right, dear."

She kissed her mother goodbye and left for the hotel to drop her car off. She parked next to Henry's Chevy, happy that he was back, then hurried toward Elm Street. The wind was warm and filled with the smell of burning.

LARRY HANDED Henry a beer from one of the deep pockets of his overcoat as they stood in the back of the crowd watching the fire, turning their backs to it when it got too hot. Everyone did, as if they were all on a spit. The crowd was almost as large as the turnout for the football game on Saturdays. They kept a respectful distance to allow the firemen to work, close enough to hear what was being said over the walkie-talkies and the radios blasting from police cars.

"My ex-wife's pregnant," Henry told Larry.

"Is it yours?"

"No."

"Could be worse, then," Larry said. He took a quarter-turn and drank from his beer.

"Could be."

"Was she fucking around while you were married?"

Henry drank his beer. "Maybe. I don't know. I don't know anything anymore."

"Crazy thing last night," Larry said. "Caroline knocked on my door when she got home from work and heard me playing one of your records. So she got a cassette and insisted I dub both of them right then and there, and she wasn't taking no for an answer. I tell you, Henry, she was crazy." He took another turn, putting his back to the fire. "So what's the story about this third album?"

"Recorded but never released. Caroline tell you about it?"

"She mentioned it. You don't have a copy?"

"Just got one today from my ex," Henry said.

"Can I tape it?"

"Sure, if it's any good. I want to hear it again first."

"Caroline's gonna want one too."

"Well, sure, same deal," Henry said, disappointed that she already had copies of the records he'd brought back. He made a quarter-turn, putting his shoulder to the fire, and took another drink.

"The boots fit?"

"How's that?" Henry said.

"The boots. Haven't you been home yet? I sent you some boots from the mill."

Henry recalled the package he'd picked up at Rachel's. "Yeah, what's that all about? You sent that? I haven't opened it yet."

Larry lit a cigarette. "In the last few weeks I started picking up some Tanner cellular phone calls on the scanner about the mill pulling out of town. Couple more calls, and I pieced together just about when they were leaving."

"So you knew. That's why you asked my shoe size the other day?"

"No risk on my part. What were they going to do— fire me?"

"Then you'd be out of a job," Henry said.

They both laughed.

"I've got a new one lined up already," Larry said, wiping his eyes.

"Really?"

"Yeah, I'm taking over for Pope. He's moving to New York next week."

"Oh?" Henry said, feeling as if someone had just snapped one of his fly rods in half in a car door, though not his favorite rod.

"Yeah. I hope it doesn't take too long to adjust to the day shift. I've been working second shift for almost twenty years now."

"Shouldn't be too bad," Henry told him, thinking now that he probably would've taken the job, despite his reservations, if Larry hadn't.

A chimney collapsed in the middle house. The crowd cheered and applauded briefly, as they would have for a touchdown, then turned back into a mass of soporific gazes and slowly turning bodies, letting the heat spread out evenly across their faces and clothes.

Henry watched the fire and thought of Kitty. Larry said something, but he was now lost in the fire with the rest of the town. It was like sitting in front of a giant hearth with a brandy in his hand, lulled and entertained by the flames.

Henry turned his back to the fire and saw Pope several yards away, smoking and sharing a pint bottle with Beverly Wall. Crazy Betty walked through the crowd in her housecoat and slippers, collecting cigarettes, and it was so warm that no one thought to take her back to the hotel. Suzie Martello and her mother had set up a refreshments table, with a coffee urn, sodas, donuts, and snacks. Though intended to give the volunteer firemen free refreshments, it made a fair profit from the bystanders.

"Do you think the Martellos are selling any marshmallows?" Larry asked, offering a wan smile.

Henry smiled and, studying the crowd, noticed Caroline watching Pope and Beverly Wall. Everybody knew Pope was dating her too, and Caroline didn't seem upset about it. She vanished into the crowd and surfaced again at the Martellos' table, where Suzie handed her a coffee. They started talking animatedly, Caroline's free arm flying erratically back and forth as if she were conducting an experimental symphony.

"Dump those beers out right now," a voice ordered

from behind them. It was Junior Dells, a special police-man—*special* meaning part time and a minor. He was twenty years old, six feet three, pear-shaped, and as soft as a wet sponge. The shadow of a mustache beneath his nose looked like the stain mold makes on bread.

Henry turned his can upside down and let the beer drain out.

"You jealous, Junior?" Larry said. "If you're thirsty, I can buy you a six-pack up to Martello's."

"Dump it," the cop said.

"I just opened it. Look around. Everybody's got a beer. You gonna arrest the whole town? I saw a Saint Bernard with a keg of brandy over by the hook and ladder. He might even have an outstanding bench warrant."

Junior Dells knocked Larry's can to the ground with his flashlight and slipped into the crowd. All Henry could see was the peak of his navy-blue campaign hat bobbing up and down. Larry pulled another beer out of his coat and offered it to Henry, who declined it.

"Why'd you dump your beer?" Larry asked him.

"Fear of cops, fear of jail."

"Fear of *Junior Dells*?" Larry said, laughing.

"All cops."

"But that was Junior Dells. Half the women I know in this town used to baby-sit him. First week on the job, he arrested a German shepherd for fighting with a smaller dog."

"He's still a cop," Henry said. "He *can* arrest you."

"Three years ago, he lettered as a towel boy for the football team."

"But not anymore."

"He'll always be Junior Dells, the towel boy who grew up to arrest a dog." Larry handed his beer to Henry while he ground out his cigarette. "He's just a little jerk with a badge."

Henry thought back to all the times alone on the road, especially toward the end, when he'd run into trouble. Small-town cops, city cops, bored cops, cops with cheating wives—it didn't matter. He seemed to attract them the way he did panhandlers in New York. There must have been something about his face, his clothes, or the way he walked that pegged him as an outsider, a target, a mark. He'd spent nights in jail for speeding, loitering, running a stop sign—anything a cop could dream up. Once, in Arizona, he was arrested for having a flat tire. After a while he learned to do whatever the cop said and say nothing in return. Alone, from out of town, he was an outsider without rights, and anything could happen. But now, back in Edson, he wished he hadn't instinctively dumped his beer out. If he'd known Junior Dells as the towel boy, as the man who arrested a dog, he would have laughed and reacted the way Larry had. He took a hit off Larry's beer, ready to go back to his apartment. "You going to be up late tonight?" he asked Larry.

"Yeah, why?"

"Tyler Beckett's on Letterman, and I wanted to see it. I'll bring the beer."

"That's a deal," Larry said.

"Okay, I'm heading back. See you later." He stopped at the Martellos' table to tell Caroline that Tyler was going to be on television. When she asked if he wanted to watch it at her apartment, he told her he'd already made plans with Larry and that Rachel was a little drunk and in a bad mood because of Lionel. "You might want to watch it with us," he said, lighting a cigarette.

"Sure," she said, eyeing the smoke. "By the way, you got two things in the mail, both express."

"Yeah, I know," he said. "Plus some boots from Larry."

"So that's who sent them," she said. "Are you going back to the hotel now?"

"Yeah. It looks like the big excitement's over for tonight."

Caroline looked around. "I guess you're right. Want some company?" She'd thought about finding her father to talk over the move, but this wasn't the right place or time.

"Sure," he said. As they cleared the crowd and the air grew cooler, he said, thinking of the cassette, "Hey, I've got a little surprise for you back at the hotel."

"Really? What is it?"

"You'll see."

"Henry!"

"Just wait." He laughed. It was a new sensation, walking with a woman almost half his age, and he liked it. They walked slowly, speculating about who might have set the fires. She thought it might've been somebody too old to start over. Her father was close to that age. Henry said it was possibly a job for hire, that the Tanners had their own houses torched by a professional from out of state.

"What on earth for? That's crazy."

"No, not really. They're never coming back, so they'd have to sell the houses. With the mill gone and no work around, what are they worth? This way they'd get the insurance money and none of the hassle."

Back at the hotel, climbing up the stairs, she told him she'd made tapes of his two records.

"Larry told me. But I've still got a surprise for you."

"What is it?"

"You'll see," he said.

"Wait a sec," she whispered, stopping at her door. "I want to get my cigarettes. Come on in."

He followed her inside. Rachel was in her bathrobe on the couch, a fresh beer in her hand, her cordless phone in the other. Her voice was lilting and flirty with whoever was on the other end. When she saw the two of them, she put her beer bottle down on the coffee table and waved by wiggling her fingers. The only light came from the television.

Caroline hurried into her bedroom for her cigarettes, and when she got back, Rachel had hung up the phone.

"That was Elliot Snow," she said, sounding very happy. Henry was surprised she wasn't slurring her words. "He's taking me to lunch tomorrow."

"Did he just call up out of the blue?" Caroline asked. "I thought he was going out with Barbara Bassell."

"Well, he is," she said. "This is just lunch. And he didn't call me, I called him. I always thought he was kind of cute."

"You called *him* up? Just like that?"

"Sure. Why not? He's very funny, you know."

Henry marveled at the scope and speed of Rachel's recuperative power. In days, Lionel Tanner would be a distant memory.

"Tyler Beckett's on Letterman tonight," Caroline said.

"Oh, I know!" Rachel said. "I've got the VCR all ready to go! I can't wait."

"We're going to watch it over at Larry's. You want to join us?"

"Thanks, but I think I'll just stay and make sure the VCR's working."

"Okay."

In Henry's apartment, Caroline noticed the records on the bed as soon as she walked in. "Henry, where'd you get these?"

"I went to see my ex-wife today. She had them."

"How was that, seeing your ex-wife?"

Henry made a face that Caroline didn't understand. "You want a drink? Beer?"

"Do you have any wine?"

"Red or white?"

"Red," she said, holding up the cassette. "What's this?"

"That's the surprise," he said. He opened the bottle of wine, then poured a bourbon for himself. "Put that in the boom box, will you?"

"What is it?"

"My third record." He set her glass of wine on the nightstand while she slipped the tape into the deck. "I don't know if it's any good or not, Caroline. I haven't heard this thing in years—since I made it, really. I was going to listen to it by myself first, but what the hell?"

HENRY SEEMED to change physically as he shifted uncomfortably in his chair, drinking, while they listened. Whenever Caroline looked up from the floor, usually after each song, she saw something different about him. After some songs he seemed larger and stronger than she knew him to be. Other times he looked ready to die of loneliness or sadness.

Henry seemed to forget she was there in the apartment. He drank and smoked and listened intently. He tried not to think of Kitty, of Kitty being pregnant, but there were several songs about her, things he'd written just before he'd quit writing. He refilled his bourbon without asking Caroline if she wanted more wine. She poured herself another glass.

When the cassette ended they both looked up, embarrassed, as if they'd been caught at something.

"It's amazing, Henry," she said, taking the lead. "I don't know what to say."

"Yeah?" He sounded tired.

"It's your best by far!"

"I kind of like it too," he said, sounding relieved. "I wish the company had."

"Well, one thing's for sure," Caroline said. "It blows Pope Johnson right out of the water."

Henry smiled. Pope had been able to learn only from his two records, and this was far beyond what he'd accomplished on those. It had been so long since he'd heard the songs that they seemed to be written by someone else, and for the first time he could step back and enjoy listening. This wasn't his *job* anymore.

"Ahh," he said slowly. "It doesn't matter." Henry looked at his watch and suggested they take some beer over to Larry's.

HENRY FELT too tired and drunk to be good company. Larry's apartment was warm with the smell of popcorn. Caroline set out beers for each of them, then put the rest in the refrigerator. They moved to the living room and talked about the fire until, at the end of the show, Letterman introduced Tyler. Larry turned up the volume with the remote. Henry, who had been shooting his mouth off about arson, was shocked into silence when she sang "Slight Rebellion off Madison." His neck felt prickly.

"This must be a new song," Caroline said. "Do you know it, Henry?"

He nodded, thinking Tyler was definitely planning to record it, that otherwise she would've wasted a valuable promotional opportunity.

After she finished the song, Tyler joined Letterman for a brief interview. "Now, that song's not on *Avenue C,* is it?" he said, holding up the CD.

"No, it's a new one," she said. "For the next album. Actually, I cowrote it with a friend of mine up in New Hampshire named Henry Corvine."

Then Letterman announced who would be on the following night, said good night, and the credits rolled.

Henry shoved his hands into his pockets and was trying to blend into the couch, when Rachel burst in. Her robe was open, and Henry stared at the cloth lilacs on her nightgown. She weaved slightly as she stood in front of the couch, glaring back at him.

"Was that you?" she demanded. "Did she mean you?"

Henry couldn't tell if she was angry or stunned.

"Yeah. We wrote that song a long time ago. It's not new."

"You know Tyler Beckett!"

"I told you he did," Caroline said. "They're old friends. Henry's a musician too."

"Was," Henry said.

"What?" Nothing was making any sense to Rachel. She shook her head, then bumped into the door on her way out.

"Did you know she was going to sing that tonight?" Larry asked.

"No. I only found out a couple days ago that she still knew it."

"It's a good song," Larry said. "Sounds real good."

"I think so too," Caroline added. "I can't believe she's going to record one of your songs. That's great! Congratulations!" She threw her arms around him and kissed him hard on the mouth. He was too drunk to be surprised.

Henry liked the way she smelled—a young smell, fresh. Caroline turned to Larry. "Henry found a cassette of his third album. We listened to it tonight. It's fantastic!"

"Yeah. I'll leave it with you tonight, Larry," Henry said. He stood up unsteadily. "I'll get it now, and then I think I better turn in."

SHE STOPPED at the store in Portsmouth on her way to work, her hangover still lurking behind her eyes. "I'm really not sure what I want exactly," she told the clerk, fidgeting with her sunglasses. "I'm hoping you can tell me."

"That's what I'm here for," the clerk said, his skinny frame towering over her. When he brushed his black, styled hair back, she thought his long, pale fingers looked like bamboo shoots.

"Well, I want to buy a set of guitar strings for a friend of mine."

"What kind?"

"I don't know. He's a folksinger." She grew increasingly uncomfortable, worried that the clerk might think she was some sort of groupie.

"That would be acoustic, then."

"Good."

"What gauge?" the clerk asked.

"What's that mean?"

"Thickness. Does he play heavy, medium, or light gauge? Does he want steel or phosphor bronze or what?"

"I just don't know." She had no idea it would be this complicated. "Never mind," she said, starting to leave.

"Does this guy work the clubs around here? Maybe I'd know who he is and what he uses."

"No," she said. "He doesn't play around here."

"So he's, like, *trying* to break into the scene here?"

"No, I don't think so," she snapped, realizing that just because she was young he thought the gift was for some beginner. "Did you see the David Letterman show last night?"

"No. I'm a bass player. I had a gig. Why?"

"It doesn't matter. Look, I've got to get going. Give me your best set of acoustic guitar strings in all three gauges. I can return the ones he doesn't want, right?"

"As long as they're not opened," the clerk said. "But would you do me a favor first?"

"What?"

"Would you take your shades off so I can see your eyes?"

"Please just ring up the sale so I can get to work."

HENRY SLEPT LATE, then spent a while going through McManus's photographs. His letter asked Henry to think again about moving to Austin.

Henry poured another cup of coffee, lit a cigarette, and opened Tyler's package. Inside was a cassette and a short note.

H—

  Here are the fragments, phrases, verses, I told you about. I'm sure there's something you can do with this stuff. Call me. Tell me you'll help.

                                               Love,
                                                 Ty

He put the cassette next to the boom box but didn't feel like playing it just yet. Instead, he thought he might walk downtown for breakfast. It was nearly two o'clock, and the lunch crowd would be finished at Judy's. He was about to leave, when the phone rang. It was Tyler.

"Hey," he said. "You were great last night! That was quite a surprise, hearing that old tune."

"Oh, yeah? Thanks, man. I told you I've been playing it quite a bit lately. It'll definitely be on the next CD."

"That's good news," Henry said.

"So what's the deal? Did you get the tape?"

"Yeah, last night," he said. "I haven't heard it yet, but I'll put it on later. I was away for a day or two."

"But what about writing with me?"

"I've thought about it, but that's as far as it's gone. Tyler, I just don't think I can do it."

"Can't or won't?"

"Can't," he said. "I'd certainly do it if I could."

"But I *know* you can. Have you at least started playing again?"

"I looked at my guitar, if that counts for anything."

"Henry, you could make a lot of money on this."

"I know." Of course he knew, but he didn't like her bringing that up. It was like Pope Johnson offering him his job and making it sound like he was doing Henry a favor.

"I'm sorry," she quickly said. "That was a little crass, wasn't it?"

"It's also true. Don't worry about it."

"Listen, Henry," she said. "Just promise me two things."

"What?"

"Promise me you'll take your guitar out and keep it out today. You don't have to play it, just keep it out."

"No. What's the other thing?"

"Promise me you'll listen to the tape today."

"No problem," he said. "That I'll definitely do."

After they talked a while longer, small talk about her family and people they knew, the last thing she said was, "Play your guitar, man."

He put on his leather jacket and left for lunch, thinking maybe he'd buy a paper and check the job listings.

It wasn't until he got downtown that he realized how foolish that idea was. Main Street was jammed with people who didn't know what to do with their time. They'd always left their houses at that time of day, and this was a momentum they couldn't break. The men stood around in small groups, looking at their watches often as if waiting for their dates to come back from the ladies' room. Any-body who wasn't on Main Street, Henry figured, was down in Portsmouth at the unemployment office.

The sky was overcast and the air was still. Henry could hear his footsteps on the sidewalk, and the quiet street struck him as odd. Nobody seemed to be talking. They stood grouped in front of the stores and shops, mostly by age and gender.

Henry ducked into Martello's for cigarettes. Debbie and Suzie stood behind the counter, but the store was empty.

"Kinda slow?" Henry said.

"Dead," Suzie said. "They're all just out there staring at the mill with these glazed-over eyes. Like they're wait-ing for something to rescue them. Well, nothing's gonna happen. Mills used to move into town before when other mills moved out, but that stuff stopped years ago."

"Yeah, it's strange," Henry said. "It's really quiet out there."

"You think they'd be pissed off or something," Suzie said.

"Well," Debbie said, "somebody did burn down the damn Tanner mansions."

"Yeah," Henry said, "but do you think the police will find out who set the fire?"

Suzie and Debbie looked at each other, surprised. "Don't think so," Debbie said. Feeling like an outsider, Henry paid for his cigarettes, said goodbye, and left. Next door, Judy's Lunch was empty too, though plenty of peo-ple were standing around outside. He bought a Boston

Globe to read while he ate a big ham and egg breakfast. When he finished, he bought the local paper and walked home to check the job listings. He found what he expected—nothing. He had no work skills, and all the unskilled jobs, he knew, would have been scooped up that morning. He looked up the phone number for the classifieds and thought about placing ads for his guns. He didn't want to sell them, but that would keep him going for a while. Somebody from Portsmouth or Exeter would have the money.

He poured a drink, lit a cigarette, and sat down on the bed. He stared at the wall, then reached under the bed for his guitar case. He opened it and set the guitar on his chair by the window. He liked looking at its slender neck and the graceful curves that gave its body an almost feminine look.

There was a knock on the door, and he heard Pope call his name. Pope never just visited, Henry thought, without wanting something, so he must've seen the Letterman show. He opened the door.

"Mr. Henry." Pope had a six-pack under his arm.

"How's it going, Mr. Pope? Want a drink?"

"Hey, your Epiphone!" Pope shouted, seeing the guitar in the chair. "Wow, I haven't seen that in years. I didn't even know you had it with you. Can I try it?"

"The strings are pretty funky. They're a couple years old. I don't think they're playable."

Pope picked up the guitar and inspected it closely. "It feels great. This neck's so thin." He set it back down. "Man, that thing plays itself. You starting to play again?"

Henry shook his head. "I might throw a new set of strings on it, though, just to see how it sounds. So you're really moving to New York, hunh?"

"Next week. I'm moving some stuff down tomorrow and then the rest of my junk on Monday. I just pumped my last gas. I'm outta here!"

Henry freshened his drink and again asked Pope if he wanted one.

"No, thanks. I've got my own here. You want one of these Molsons?"

"You find a place already?"

"Yeah," Pope said, laughing. "Although I can't say as I've seen it. I'm gonna room with one of my old college roommates."

"I didn't know you went to college."

"I never did finish." Pope ripped a beer from the six-pack and opened it. "You know, I've got a box of strings back home. Why don't you take a set?"

"No, but thanks."

"Really, you should."

Something didn't feel right to Henry. It was as if Pope was defining half the terms of a swap. "Well, you use medium gauge, and that's too much tension. I've got to string it up with lights, or the neck will warp."

"Oh." Pope pulled on his earlobe.

They drank and talked about New York. Pope had already lined up a day job painting apartments with his roommate. Henry asked if he knew anybody else down there, and immediately regretted the question.

"Not really," Pope said. "Hey, maybe y'all could help.

You must know some people in New York who could give me a hand. You know, introduce me to other people, show me the ropes. God, that would save me from running around in circles, spinning my wheels."

Henry lit a cigarette and crossed his arms. He locked eyes with Pope and spoke very slowly. "I imagine I do know some people."

"Great! You know, what would be a big help is Tyler Beckett's number."

"Did you like the show last night?"

"Oh, Letterman? Yeah, she was great, wasn't she? How do you happen to know her?"

"I've known her for years."

"I had no idea. When did you start writing with her?"

Henry shrugged and didn't answer. He bit down on his cigarette with his lips, flattening the filter.

Pope pulled a notebook from his rear pocket and a pen from his shirt pocket. "Well, I just have this feeling she'd like my songs."

"She probably would."

"So what's her number?"

"It's unlisted," Henry said, "so don't give it out to anyone." Then he made up a number on the spot.

"I won't, promise. You know Dave Van Ronk?"

"Sure. You want his number?"

"Yeah."

Henry got up and picked up his address book from his desk—an unfinished door on two sawhorses—and read off another fictitious number for Pope to dutifully copy down. He almost asked if Pope wanted any others. How about Prince Charles or Mother Teresa?

Pope did ask about several other producers and per-formers, for whom Henry made up a half-dozen more numbers.

"But I wouldn't contact anybody until you've actually moved to the city. They're busy, and they might want to see you right then, and it wouldn't look good if you were still in New Hampshire. Sometimes you only get one chance with these people."

"That's a good idea," Pope said, standing up. "Man, thanks for all this. I should get back and start packing. I can't wait to get to the city. I feel like I'm loaded for bear now." He wrote out his new address and number and ripped it out of the notebook for Henry.

"Take care, Mr. Pope."

"You too, Mr. Henry. And thanks again."

Henry listened to him walk down the hall, then picked up the address from the table and threw it in the trash. Loaded for bear, he thought, laughing to himself.

RACHEL WAS a few minutes late for work, but business was slow and it didn't matter. Caroline asked her how her lunch date had gone.

"Oh, it was good!" Rachel said. "We just laughed and laughed. He's taking me out Sunday."

"Really? But what about Barbara Bassell? He's still going out with her, isn't he?"

"Who knows," Rachel answered, then paused. "You

know, I still can't believe Henry's really *friends* with Tyler Beckett! And he never said a word, can you imagine? Have you ever talked to him about it?"

"Not really. I just found out a couple days ago."

"Do you think he could, like, get us tickets when she comes to Boston or Portland? I'll bet he could get us backstage! Wouldn't that be cool?"

"We should get to work," Caroline said. She didn't want to talk about any of this. Her father had called the apartment that morning to say he expected her to move with them once they found a house. She explained she had her own life, that it was here in Edson, but he insisted. She refused, he demanded, and she practically hung up on him.

After putting the phone down, Caroline had opened a window and lit a cigarette with trembling hands. She'd never defied her father before. Not like that. She had started smoking, but that was like sneaking something, not putting her foot down and saying no. Maybe, she thought, she'd had the power to make her own decisions about her life for a long time but didn't know it until she was forced to do so. Then she wondered how much power she actually had, and what she'd do if her father tried to make her move.

But she couldn't discuss this with Rachel. Besides, all Rachel wanted to talk about was Tyler Beckett and Henry.

"I just can't believe he used to be a musician," she said. "What does he sound like?"

"Kind of like Pope, only lower," Caroline said. "And sort of older."

"Pope?"

"Actually, Pope sounds like Henry. He grew up listening to Henry's records, and a lot of the songs he sings are Henry's."

"Really?" Rachel asked. "But do you think Henry and Tyler ever went out?"

"Oh, I don't know." She recalled Henry saying they never were lovers, but she didn't want to tell Rachel.

"You know," Rachel said, "I think Henry's kind of attractive in an older-man sort of way."

"What?" Caroline said, alarmed. "Since when?"

"I mean, how could you miss it? It's like this guy with a secret past or something. That's kind of exciting."

"You were making fun of him the other day. A Sally Fields film festival—isn't that what you said?"

"I never made fun of him," Rachel said. "I just never knew that he had this other life before he came here. I think that's very sexy, having a secret past that nobody knows anything about."

"He doesn't have a secret past," Caroline said. "It's just that nobody remembers what he used to do."

WHEN HENRY heard Larry unlock his door, he walked over and asked if he'd copied his third album yet.

"Yeah," Larry said, "and it's great. I think it's your best. How come it was never released?" He took the original cassette off the bookcase and handed it to Henry.

"Well, what it was, they just didn't know how to market it. Probably didn't think it would sell. Anyway, I'm glad you like it. Listen, Larry, you've got my first two records, right?"

"Yeah."

"Do you think you could make me copies like you did for Caroline? I don't have a record player."

"Sure. No problem."

"Thanks. See you later."

Back in his apartment, Henry was anxious to listen to his third album again. It had been a relief not to hate it. If there were mistakes on it, and he was sure there were, they hadn't jumped out at him. Maybe the second time around it would be different.

He'd surprised himself the night before when he played it with Caroline there. Well, he thought, he wanted to hear it and couldn't very well kick her out, nor did he want to. As he slipped it into the boom box, he saw Tyler's tape on the nightstand and promised himself he'd get to it that night.

RACHEL AND CAROLINE sat at the bar with the other waitresses, counting their tips and having a drink.

"Is Pope really moving to New York?" Rachel asked as she folded the bills and slipped them into her purse.

"That's what he says."

"When?"

"I don't know," Caroline said. "Soon was all he said."

"What are you going to do?"

"Start seeing somebody else, I guess."

"Aren't you upset?" Rachel took a rubber band from her purse and pulled her hair back in a ponytail.

"Not really. He was seeing other girls too, so it's not like we were an item. I mean, I'll miss him, but I'm not exactly heartbroken."

"But you weren't going out with anybody else, right?"

"Right." She didn't feel like telling Rachel how she felt about Henry.

"I could fix you up with somebody," Rachel said.

Caroline knew she meant one of her many ex-boyfriends. Maybe a few months before, she might've tried one or two, but not now. She wanted to get home and hoped Henry was still awake so she could give him the guitar strings. "No, thanks," she told Rachel. "Not right now."

"Okay."

"But tell me something. Were you nervous when you asked Elliot Snow out last night?"

"What do you mean?"

"Were you nervous? What would you have done if he said no?"

Rachel looked puzzled. "I'd have called somebody else. There are plenty of guys out there, and somebody would've wanted to take me out to lunch. Why?"

"I was just wondering," Caroline said. "I've never asked a guy out."

Rachel thought for a second, nodding her head. "That doesn't surprise me."

"Have you ever been turned down?"

"Sure."

"But wasn't it humiliating?" Caroline asked.

"For about two seconds. I mean, some people like you and some don't. It's always going to be that way, and there's nothing you can do about it. So when somebody isn't interested, I just move on."

"But what if you're really crazy about somebody and he doesn't feel the same?"

"You're not talking about Pope, so who is it, Caroline?"

"It's nobody," Caroline said, hiding her face behind her drink.

"Well, maybe you should just ask Mr. Nobody out sometime and see how things go," Rachel said.

IT WAS TWO in the morning when Henry woke up. The space heater was still on, and his clothes were damp with sweat. He got up from the bed and went to the bathroom to splash water on his face. He knew he wouldn't be able to get back to sleep until five at least. But so what if his whole sleep schedule was thrown off for a couple days? What did it matter? All he had to do was run the ad for his guns and field the occasional phone call. He wiped his face dry, lit a cigarette, and sat back down on the bed. He wanted to call somebody on the phone, anybody. He poured a bourbon, thinking maybe he could drink himself back to sleep. Two o'clock here meant it was eleven on the West Coast, but who did he know out there who would be sitting around on a Friday night? His studio apartment seemed cavernous in the orange light from the space heater, the streetlamp down below in the parking lot shining weakly through his shades.

He took his cassette out of the boom box, put Tyler's in, and sat back in his chair. He heard Rachel and Caroline walking down the hall, talking, then Tyler's first piece. It was one verse, a quatrain repeated six times, as if she was trying to siphon additional lyrics out of thin air, trying to add something to the four rickety poles that propped up the whole structure. He liked the melody but knew the song cried out for a bridge. It ended abruptly, as if something had interrupted her, and the next fragment started, a fast minor-key progression. Henry waited for the lyrics to come in, but they never did. It was just a chord progression, with Tyler humming a nondescript melody around the pedal points. The lyrics could be anything.

Caroline rapped on his door. Henry recognized her polite knock, and besides, Rachel wasn't likely to stop by.

"It's open, Caroline," he called, stopping the cassette.

"How'd you know it was me?" she asked, opening the door.

"Come on in."

"Can I have a cigarette in here?"

"You can do anything you want in here," Henry said.

Caroline shut the door behind her. She sat down on the bed and took the cigarettes out of her purse. She lit one and took a quick drag. "God, what a day!"

"You want something to drink?"

"Hang on," she said, leaving her cigarette in the ashtray and hurrying out the door. She returned holding a vodka bottle. "Have you got any cranberry juice?"

"Nope. Only tonic and grapefruit."

"Would you make me a vodka tonic?" she asked, handing him the fifth. Then she noticed his guitar in the chair. "Henry! Have you been playing?"

"No, just looking at it."

"It's beautiful." She moved closer and saw that the strings were brown. Smiling, she walked back to the bed and took her cigarette from the ashtray. Henry handed her the vodka and tonic, then sat down at his desk.

"I've got something for you," she said, reaching into her purse.

"Oh, that reminds me," Henry said. "Larry made that tape for you."

"That was fast," she said, handing him the three sets of guitar strings. "I hope one of these is the right gauge."

"What's this?" he said, slowly fanning them out like playing cards. He pulled out one set and put the others on his desk. "This is what I used to play. What's this all about?"

"Oh, I don't know. I was in a music store today and I happened to remember you saying your strings were too rusty to play, so I picked some up for you."

There was another knock on the door. "Hey, you two! Can I come in?" Rachel called.

Caroline jumped up and rushed into the bathroom with her cigarette. Henry heard her flush the toilet and run water in the sink.

Rachel walked in. "What are you two up to?" she said, waving her hand in front of her face. "God, it's smoky in here."

"Yeah, it kind of is," Henry said. He got up from the desk and opened a window. "Was the smoke bothering you, Caroline?" he asked when she came out of the bathroom. He smiled so only she could see. "You should've said something."

She smiled back and sat down on the bed. "That's fine, Henry."

"Hey, what are you guys drinking?" Rachel asked.

"Caroline's having a vodka tonic," Henry said, "and I'm drinking bourbon. There's also some beer and wine. What would you like?"

"I'd love a vodka tonic," Rachel said.

Henry got up to make her drink, and Caroline patted the bed beside her. "Have a seat, Rachel," she said, mostly wanting her to leave so she could smoke and have another drink, working up her courage to ask Henry out to lunch.

"This is a cozy little apartment, Henry," Rachel said when he came back with her drink.

"That's right, you've never been over here before."

"It's, like, the perfect bachelor's apartment." Rachel tasted her drink. "Don't you think so, Caroline?"

"I've always liked this place." Caroline thought maybe she should just light up. If Rachel didn't like it, Caroline could find her own place once her parents left town, and she could smoke whenever she liked.

"So what brings you out tonight, Rachel?" Henry asked.

"I don't know. I'm not tired yet and there's nothing

on TV. It just got a little lonely over there, so I thought I'd come visit. I'm not interrupting anything, am I?"

"We were just talking," Henry said.

"Is that your guitar, Henry?" she asked, and he nodded. "Could you play us something?"

"He doesn't play anymore," Caroline told her.

Rachel crossed her legs and let the hem of her skirt ride well up her thigh. "Sing that one Tyler Beckett sang last night. You wrote it with her, right? You must remember how to play that."

Henry had wondered how long it would be before she mentioned Tyler Beckett.

"I told you, he doesn't play anymore."

"He doesn't play anymore," Rachel said slowly, drawing the words out. "How can you write songs if you don't play an instrument?" She saw the packs of strings on the desk and picked them up. "What are these for, then?"

"Caroline bought them for me," Henry said.

"Oh, really?" Rachel said, turning to Caroline. "You bought Henry guitar strings?"

"I happened to be in a music store, and his old strings are rusty," she said. "It's just in case he wants to start playing again."

"I'm sure it is," Rachel said. "Henry, where can I get your CDs? Caroline says you've got two."

"I don't have any CDs. They only came out on LP and cassette."

"So where can I get them?"

"Well, Caroline has copies."

"You do?" Rachel said sharply. "You never told me that."

"You can borrow them, Rachel."

"Thanks. So, Henry, tell us about Tyler Beckett. What's she like?"

"Ah, let's talk about something else. I'm a little burned out on that subject about now. Some other time."

"Promise?"

"Yeah, fine," he said. "I'll tell you everything you'll ever need to know about Tyler Beckett."

"I can't wait," Rachel said. "How about tomorrow over lunch? My treat."

Caroline's face darkened as she glared at Rachel, her eyes like two suns flaming their way through midday storm clouds.

"I don't think I can tomorrow," Henry said. "My whole sleep schedule's so screwed up I won't be awake in time for lunch."

"Well, some other time," Rachel said.

"Fine."

"Soon?"

"Yeah, fine."

Rachel talked about work at the restaurant while she finished her drink, then she yawned. "Well, I guess I'm getting tired. I'm going to bed. How about you, Caroline?"

"I'm not tired," Caroline said. "Why don't you go on ahead?"

"Okay, I will," Rachel said. "Good night, Henry. Thanks for the drink."

Caroline had a cigarette lit before Rachel even reached their apartment. "I thought she'd never leave," she whispered.

Henry lit one to join her. "I don't know why you keep hiding these things from everybody. It's no big deal."

"You're right," she said. "I don't know why either."

"Personally, I think you should stop while you can, but that's up to you."

"I know." She sighed. "I'm not keeping you from anything, am I?"

"No, not at all. You want another drink?"

"Sure, if you're having one."

They sat smoking and talking, and after the second drink she asked Henry out to dinner on Sunday.

"That'd be great," he said. "Where do you want to go?"

"I really haven't thought about it," she said, astonished that he'd said yes. "I don't know. Anywhere you want. We can figure it out later."

Finally she said good night and drifted back to her apartment.

In the kitchen she ran into Rachel and asked, "If you were taking somebody out for a quiet dinner, where would you go?"

"Who are you going with?" Rachel asked, refilling an empty Evian bottle with tap water.

"Henry."

"*Henry?*" She capped her bottle. "I don't know where I'd take him. You two are really going out?"

"Yeah. I just want to find the right place."

"I wouldn't know where to take him," Rachel said. "No place around here, that's for sure. I mean, he writes songs with Tyler Beckett. Some place in Boston. That's where I'd go."

"But I don't know anywhere in Boston."

"I'll think about it," Rachel said, drying her hands, "but I've got to get some sleep. Let's talk in the morning."

THE PHONE woke Caroline from a deep sleep late that morning. "Where's Stephen?" her mother shrieked.

"What?" She didn't recognize her mother's voice.

"Stephen's gone!"

"What?"

"I told you. Stephen's gone. He ran away!"

Caroline suddenly propped herself up onto one elbow. "Where are you?"

"At home. We just got home. Stephen left a note saying he wasn't moving to Newport and didn't want to end up working at the mill. He said he was leaving, but he didn't say where to."

"Did he say anything else?"

"Just that he'd call as soon as he settled in somewhere," her mother said. "Where do you think he went?"

"I have no idea, Mom." Now that the news was sinking in, Caroline was just as alarmed. "Where was Harold when Stephen left?"

"He was evidently spending the night with that Louise girl," she said.

"You want me to come over?" Caroline asked.

"Of course I want you to. We've got to find him!"

"I'll be right there." Her cigarettes were still in her

purse. She stuffed a towel at the bottom of her bedroom door, pulled out the pack and lit up, then wrapped herself in her bathrobe and opened the window. She turned the little fan on. The breeze that blew in on her was clean and cooled by the snow, but the day was warm and sunny. The weather was going crazy, she thought—warm one day, freezing the next, then back again. Water dripped from roofs everywhere, and she could see patches of washed-out brown grass through the holes in the snow. The longer she stayed at the window, the more it seemed like early spring rather than November. The air seemed to hold the promise of gentler days ahead, and she savored the moment because she knew that the days ahead would be anything but gentle. Spring was always something fought for and hard won.

Caroline lit a second cigarette and tried to imagine where her brother had gone. She hoped it was someplace different, someplace big—New York City, California, Texas. She prayed he wouldn't set off for another world and three months later turn up penniless in a Super 8 in Keene.

"CORVINE!" the desk clerk called out. His cheeks were sucked in, and his chin was fuzzy with gray stubble.

Henry stopped at the lobby door. "What?" He wasn't fully awake.

"You got a package. More overnight mail. I had to *sign* for it." He made this sound like a great favor.

"Yeah, life's tough." Henry walked over to the desk. It was from Tyler. What now? he thought.

"You're way overdressed," the clerk told him. "It's like September out there."

Henry opened the envelope, and two slips of paper fell out. One was a letter; the other was a cashier's check for five thousand dollars. He sat down on the lobby couch next to Crazy Betty and looked at the check for a long time before reading the letter.

Dear Henry,

   Here's a little advance on the royalties for "Slight Rebellion." It's going to make us both a lot of money, and I thought you might be able to use some a little early. At least you won't have to pump gas all winter. Call me when you've heard the tape. I know you can do this. Besides, it'll be fun, man.

                                         Love,

                                              Tyler

He pulled out a pack of cigarettes, took one for himself, and gave one to Crazy Betty. He almost gagged on the sour smell of a human being decomposing while still alive. His hand was trembling, and he didn't know if it was from the check or just the whiskey catching up with him. He briefly wondered if it would be easier to quit smoking or drinking. He decided that drinking would be easier to give up, and that he wasn't about to. He'd been heading outside for coffee and breakfast, but he returned to his apartment and poured himself a bourbon, which went down easily after the first swallow.

He heard Rachel walking around in her bedroom and turned on the clock radio to drown her out. Somebody was singing a song about food on the country station. Henry snapped the power off. What a ridiculous thing to write about, he thought. Tomatoes! Jesus Christ. He'd listened to Tyler's cassette over and over until dawn, and he played it now without following it closely. He ground out the stub of his cigarette and lit another, then picked up the check again. Five thousand dollars. It was the most money he'd seen in a long time. He could live in Edson for almost a year on that. He could do a lot of things. He could re-record and release the songs on his third album. Or he could move somewhere else, maybe Austin, and start all over, doing something else. Austin was even cheaper than Edson. He knew that cashing the check would unofficially obligate him to write with Tyler, even though it was money that eventually was coming to him anyway. What she was doing was floating him a loan that put him in her debt. He was very glad it was Saturday afternoon and the bank was closed. He had until Monday to decide.

His apartment felt hot and stuffy. The bourbon had bored a hunger into his stomach. He wanted to get out for a walk and some breakfast. He liked to think things over while walking, so it was time to walk some laps.

Downtown, this was a quiet Saturday like any other. Even when the mill still operated, this wasn't a workday. Men were out in the woods hunting or in the clubs watching football or working on things around the house or washing cars. The warm air seemed oddly uninvited, and by late afternoon it disappeared, not to come back for a long time. Gray clouds rolled in by four o'clock, clouds heavy with snow.

CAROLINE'S MOTHER was on the phone with Stephen's friends, but none of them knew where he might have gone. Her father sat at the kitchen table, half listening while he drank a cup of coffee. Caroline poured herself a big mug.

"The cops won't lift a finger, because he's supposedly an adult," he told her. "But this doesn't strike me as any kind of adult behavior."

"Can I see the note he left?" Caroline asked.

"It's on the counter by your mother. You smell like you've been smoking."

"I was over at my neighbor Henry's apartment. He smokes all the time."

"What were you doing over there?" he said.

She didn't reply. Instead, she took the note back to the kitchen table and read it quickly. "He didn't say much, did he?"

"I'm going to wring his neck when I see him."

"No you're not, Harry," Caroline's mother said, joining them at the table.

"I sure as hell am. This is the worst possible time to pull a stunt like this."

"Where do you think he is, Caroline?" her mother asked.

"I have no idea."

"You're his sister!" her father said.

"I don't know! How should I know where he went? He didn't tell me anything. I wish I knew."

"He *didn't?*" Her father made this sound like an accusation. He pushed his empty coffee cup toward Caroline's mother. She picked it up, refilled it, and brought it back to him.

"I told you I don't know," Caroline said. "Where's Harold?"

"He's out looking for your brother," her father said, "doing what you should be doing."

"I don't know where to start. You've talked to all his friends, right? I'll drive around the streets, if that's what you want."

"Speaking of starting," he said. "Marjorie, can you think of anyone else to call?"

She shook her head.

"Then maybe you should start packing." Then he turned to Caroline. "And you might help your mother. We're moving on Monday. You can pack up your own apartment later."

"I'll help Mom, but I'm not packing up my things," Caroline said. "I'm not going anywhere."

"I just rented a four-bedroom house. You're going."

"Dad, I told you I wasn't moving."

He slapped her face. "I told you I wasn't about to let this family break up, and I'm not about to let *you* break it up! It's bad enough I let you move into that run-down dump with that trash from Cape Cod!" He pounded the table with his fist and spilled half his coffee. "Now look what you made me do!" He jumped back from the table as Caroline's mother sopped it up with paper towels.

"You hit me!" Caroline said, holding her cheek, sliding her chair away from the table. "I have to go. I have to get ready for work."

"You get back here and help your mother!"

"No! I have to go. I have a job!"

"Get back here!" he ordered.

She didn't start crying until she was in her car.

HENRY AND NAPPY Baudette shot eight-ball in the Polish Club for most of the afternoon. By the time Henry started home, it was dark and snowing heavily.

Back in his apartment, though it was still early, he undressed and put on his bathrobe. He poured a drink and took a partridge out of the refrigerator. He was hungry again, and partridge with wild rice sounded about right. The phone rang while he was turning on the oven. He answered, thinking it might be Tyler.

"Hi, Henry. I thought I heard you come in," Rachel said. "I called in sick this afternoon, but now it turns out

I'm all right. I haven't seen anybody all day and could use some company. I've got some Jack Daniel's," she added. "So why don't you come over for a drink?"

Her voice was soft, and Henry was just drunk enough to play along with her.

"I'm in my bathrobe," he said.

"Me too."

"Okay, I'll be over in five minutes." He lit a cigarette and sat down on the bed. It wasn't like Rachel to invite him over, he thought. Maybe she needed a jar opened or something. Whatever. It was worth the price of a drink. He picked up his clothes from the floor and dressed again.

Rachel greeted him with a drink already poured. "Hi," she said as she handed it to him, then let him follow her inside. She was wearing makeup and perfume and jewelry. In the living room, she turned around and looked at him. "Well, if you're dressed," she said, "I'll change too."

"You look pretty dressed to me."

"Oh, I was thinking about going out, but I stopped halfway. It's snowing again, and I just want to stay in. Make yourself at home. I'll be out in a minute."

He sat down on the divan and sipped his drink. The lamp across the room was turned to dim, and the stereo was playing softly. Rachel returned wearing a snug V-neck sweater and a black skirt. She smiled as she went into the kitchen to pour herself a glass of wine.

"You can use that saucer on the coffee table for an ashtray, Henry," she called.

"Really?" She had never let anybody smoke in the apartment before, as far as he knew. "Sure, one or two won't hurt," she said, sitting down next to him. She tasted her wine. "I want you to be comfortable."

When she crossed her legs and turned toward him, Henry noticed how close she was. "So, how come you called in sick?"

"I just didn't feel like working. Is your drink okay?"

"Well, it's kind of hard to screw up bourbon and ice."

She laughed and tapped her index finger against her temple. "Yeah, *duh*. Oh, I was listening to your tape all afternoon."

And what did you think? he wanted to say. Then he caught a whiff of her perfume and he liked it. His ex-wife used to wear it, and suddenly he was angry that he couldn't remember its name. "So I guess you want to hear about Tyler Beckett," he said.

"Not if you don't want to talk about it. Just relax, drink up. There's plenty of bourbon. I'm glad to have some company." She took a sip of wine.

He lit a cigarette. He had a check for five thousand dollars in his wallet. He hadn't been with a woman since his marriage broke up. Now here he was in a pretty woman's living room. When he finished his drink, Rachel took the glass from his hand and refilled it. They talked and drank. Each time she returned with a fresh drink, she moved closer to him. She began to touch his thigh when she emphasized certain words in the conversation.

"Oh, listen!" she said, going over to turn up the stereo. "The Righteous Brothers," she shouted. "I love this song! My parents always played it on this oldies album they had.

Come on, Henry, let's dance." She took both his hands
and pulled him up.

"Unchained Melody" was the first song Henry had
ever danced to—in the seventh grade, with a girl named
Shelley. He didn't really know how to dance then, and he
just kind of slid his shoes along the floor so he wouldn't
step on her feet.

Rachel put her hands around his neck and moved close
to him. She pressed her breasts against him and rested her
head on his shoulder. He loved the way she smelled. He
closed his eyes and began to get erect, and when she
rocked her hips against his he knew she could feel him
growing large.

"Henry?" she said softly in his ear. "Remember that
lingerie you picked out for Caroline the other day?"

"I think so."

"I got an outfit like it for myself."

"Yeah?"

"And I'm wearing it."

"Really?"

"You want to see?"

"Nah," he said. "I don't think so."

"What?" Surprised, she pulled away to look at his
face.

"No. I don't want you to model it for me. I know
what you're thinking, and I know I'd greatly enjoy it. But
I also know I couldn't possibly afford it in the long
run."

"Afford it? Afford what? What are you talking
about?"

Henry kept dancing. Everything's some sort of deal, he thought. "Such as, where were you two days ago?"

"What do you mean?"

"I *think* that was before the Letterman show."

"Don't think." She pressed her hips against his. "Just do me. Take me. Any way you want." She rocked her hips. "We both know you want me. And I want you."

"Dip," he announced clownishly, bending her over backward.

"What are you doing?" she said, irritated.

"Gotta go," Henry said, breaking away as the song ended. "Thanks for the dance."

CAROLINE MENTALLY cataloged every article of clothing in her closet as she waited tables, narrowing her choice to five outfits. The next morning she'd try each one on to see what looked best. She'd already decided on the restaurant, a tiny inn three towns over, where they wouldn't run into anyone they knew.

HENRY LISTENED to Tyler's tape over and over while he lay on the bed and stared at the ceiling, wondering if he'd done the right thing in turning Rachel down. Maybe McManus was right about putting his marriage behind him, finding somebody, anybody, and just having a randy old time of it. It didn't have to make sense.

Henry got up and brought his guitar and the new strings back to the bed. This was as good a time as any, he thought, to see how it sounded. He had to do something. Looking at his old Epiphone was like finding his old high school yearbook up in the attic. There were nicks and sweat stains and beer stains and scrapes on its face, but it still was elegant—like a beautiful forty-year-old woman with one tooth slightly awry. He remembered where each nick and scrape came from, though the beer and sweat stains had just seemed to happen when he wasn't looking. He picked the guitar up by the neck and held it in front of him. The G string was so shot and rusted it was unraveling.

He put the guitar down, slid the case from under the bed, and took out his electronic tuner. He flipped it on, but as he'd expected, the battery was dead. He tossed the tuner on the bed. Martello's was still open. He could get a new battery there, but he sure as hell could still tune a fucking guitar by ear, couldn't he?

Henry got up and poured himself a drink, then took it back to the bed, lit a cigarette, and unwound the bass E string. Something felt right and familiar, as if he was performing a long-neglected ritual. He didn't even have to think about what he was doing. He kept Tyler's tape on as a reference while he changed strings. He knew she was tuned up to concert pitch, and he matched his guitar to hers. Once he'd changed all six strings and was tuned, he began picking along with the tape. After a while he realized that some of Tyler's chord progressions were things he'd heard her play years before, raw ideas she'd never been able to develop. This hadn't occurred to him while he was just listening.

Then the tape came up on the melodic fragment he'd been struck by the night before. He easily figured out what she was playing, but his fingers weren't fast or accurate enough anymore. Many of the notes buzzed against the fingerboard or came in a quarter beat late. Soon the fingertips of his left hand throbbed slightly and felt warm. He turned the tape off and played the fragment slower, by himself, over and over. He put a capo on the second fret, which raised the key a step but lowered the action to make it easier on his fingers. He didn't notice the empty bourbon glass and stopped only to take a drag on his cigarette or light another one. He inverted chords, changing accents and root positions, looking for a place to jump into an unexpected middle eight to break it up, but it was the kind of repetitious progression where the bridge could pop up anywhere.

The hotel was quiet for a Saturday night, but in strong gusts of wind it creaked like an old ship, and the electric light wobbled overhead. Henry played until his fingertips were swollen and burning. He knew the next day would be worse, but eventually the calluses would build up. When he put the guitar away, he left the plush-lined case open against the far wall so he would see it first thing in the morning.

DRIVING HOME in the snowstorm was even more drain-
ing than her shift at the Pilot Inn. Another four inches had
fallen, and it was still coming down heavily. The wind
seemed unable to make up its mind—blowing her car one
way and then the other, sometimes disappearing for minutes at a time. Henry's car was in the lot when she got
home, but his light was off.

Caroline was glad she hadn't had a drink after work,
but she wanted one now. A bottle of wine was open on
the kitchen counter, so she poured the last few inches into
a glass. She stopped, puzzled by the smell of cigarette
smoke, then took the wine back to her bedroom. It was
too cold and raw outside to open the window, but Caroline
put a towel on the floor to cover the crack beneath the
door and lit a cigarette. As she hung out her five outfits
on moldings, bookcases, and closet doors, she wondered
again about the cigarette smell in the kitchen.

IN THE MORNING, he put the coffee water on and
showered while it heated. After toweling off, he made a
mug to sip at while he dressed. Then he took his guitar

out of its case and sat down on the bed, gingerly fingering the fingerboard. It hurt more than he'd thought it would. The strings themselves felt like red-hot wires. He lit a cigarette and hunched over the guitar to play Tyler Beckett's fragment almost inaudibly, his left hand barely touching the strings. He drank his coffee and smoked as he played, and the hours passed by unnoticed.

Then he saw it—the middle eight bars, the bridge—and where it would go. A simple transition involving two passing chords, it seemed so obvious that he couldn't believe he hadn't seen it the night before. His heart pounded and his hands felt unsteady as the melody practically dictated itself. Ignoring the burning in his fingertips, he played it until he'd memorized it, then went through the whole song over and over. Everything fit together well, he thought.

He played a while longer, then ran out of cigarettes. Setting his guitar down on the bed, he blew on his fingertips, thinking maybe that was enough for the day. He took three aspirin for the pain, in case they could reach all the way to his fingers, then put on his coat and walked downtown to Martello's.

Debbie had the Sunday paper spread out over the counter and was reading bits of articles between customers.

"How's business?" Henry asked.

"Not too bad, considering," she said. "Weekdays are still off some, but with people standing around downtown all day, somebody's gotta buy something. What do you need—cigarettes?"

"Yeah, two of each, please. That and a nine-volt alkaline."

"Cold out?"

"Real nasty," Henry said.

"Supposed to get freezing rain tonight," Debbie said, looking down at the paper.

"Well, it's sleeting now," Henry said flatly. Walking home, he hummed the melody to the bridge. He wanted to play some more, but his fingers were still hurting.

Back at the hotel, he found a note from Caroline tacked to his door.

Dear Henry,

If it's okay with you I thought we'd go to the Olde Carriage Inn. Is seven o'clock good for you? Give me a call when you get in.

Caroline

He'd forgotten all about dinner. His watch said three o'clock. Henry unlocked his door and went inside, then lit a cigarette and poured some coffee. It wasn't that he didn't want to see Caroline. He enjoyed her company more than anyone else's lately, and she was attractive in a strangely innocent way, maybe because she was so young. He just didn't want to go out that night. It felt as if something important was being interrupted. Then, just as suddenly, he felt ashamed. His fingers hurt, and he really wasn't going to get much work done that night, and he hadn't been out with anyone for so long. He shook his head. It wasn't as though he'd suddenly become a musician again overnight.

Noticing that he had two calls on his phone machine, he played them back while he soaked his fingertips in cold water under the faucet.

"Hey, baby," Tyler said. "I hope you got my little surprise, so cash it and have yourself a night on the town—as much as you can up there. It's Sunday afternoon. Call me tonight. See ya."

"Yeah," Henry muttered.

"Mr. Henry, it's Mr. Pope. I'm back in town. I'm doing my final hoot at the Millhouse, so drop by if you can. I'd like to get a chance to thank you and say goodbye in person. Drinks are on me all night."

Sure, Henry thought. That would make things even. He turned the water off and dried his hand, then called Caroline. Rachel answered.

"It's Henry. Is Caroline there?"

"She's in the shower."

"Would you tell her I called?"

"Well," she said, "I'm just going out."

"So leave her a note."

"Look—I'm not your goddamn messenger." She slammed the phone down, and a minute later he heard her stomping down the hall.

Henry called Tyler and got her machine. "I'm not saying yes to anything," he said, "but my fingertips are as raw as hell. I think you've got some great ideas. I don't know if I can do anything with them, but *you've* got some great ideas. I'm here until seven tonight, then I should be around all day tomorrow."

"You started playing again, Corvine!" Tyler shouted, picking up the phone.

"Screening calls, eh?"

"No. I was in the bathroom, you peckerwood. So tell me about this. You started playing again, didn't you?"

"Well, not exactly. I mean, this girl down the hall bought me a set of strings, and last night I got so bored and pissed off that I restrung the Epiphone and just started fucking around. You know, nothing serious."

"The proverbial girl down the hall—that sounds interesting."

"Well, yeah," he said. "She's real nice, but she's only twenty-one."

"Do you help her with her homework?"

"You should see her in her cheerleader's outfit."

Tyler laughed. "You're crazy, Henry. So have you done anything with the tape yet?"

"Not really. I just picked up the guitar again, though I might have an idea or two."

"That's great! When do you think you can get down to Danbury?"

"Ty, I told you. I really don't know if I can do this. I don't know. Maybe I can, but who knows? Let me play around with it a bit longer. That'll give me a better idea."

"Sure, man," she said. "But you know I've really got to get going on this."

"Yeah, I know."

"And besides, it'll be fun hanging out together. And you bring your little string buyer if you want."

Henry recalled what he'd said to Rachel the night before—about not being able to afford it in the long run.

Now it wasn't the musical part of Tyler's deal that frightened Henry. Tones and intervals, harmonies and rhythms, were challenging but unthreatening, things to work with and shape, just sounds. They weren't human, and weren't as serious for Henry as lyrics. Working with Tyler meant writing lyrics as well—and that involved dredging up the past, especially his most recent past, and turning all that unpleasantness into stories to put out for public consumption. This wasn't anybody's idea of fun, but it was the only way he knew how to write. He was still too close to the divorce to see it with any perspective, and why inspect the wound so soon after surgery if you're not the doctor?

"Yeah, well, look," Henry said. "I'll call you tomorrow."

"Okay. Hey, I'm glad you picked up your old Epiphone again. How'd it feel?"

"It felt fine until it became obvious my calluses are long gone and my fingers are made of lead."

Tyler chuckled. "Never should have stopped, man."

"I'll call you tomorrow," Henry said, hanging up. Never should have stopped. Yeah, and never should've had a record company that wouldn't release my last fucking record. Christ! Sucking hard on his cigarette, he took Tyler's tape out of the boom box and put in his last album. As he listened, he felt the blisters blooming on his fingertips. And he realized it didn't matter that he liked the way it sounded, or that he'd stayed true to his intentions, because nobody had ever heard it.

SHE HAD FORGOTTEN about the little bag tucked away in her underwear drawer. Now in her bathrobe, with a towel wrapped around her head, she dug out the black lace garter belt and matching bra she'd bought with Rachel. She inspected them as if she were still thinking of buying them, then stuffed everything back into the bag and put it away. After drying her hair, she was trying on the outfit she liked best when Henry phoned.

"Hi!" she said and then cringed, thinking she sounded too enthusiastic.

"Seven's fine," Henry said, "but have you looked outside? It's nasty already and supposed to get worse."

She felt a twinge of disappointment. "Well, my Civic's great in the snow. I think it'll be all right."

"Sure. And if not, we can just make it some other night."

"Oh, okay."

"I'll come by at seven, then," he said.

The outfit she'd picked out was slightly conservative and made her look a little older, which she liked. She spun around slowly in front of her mirror, wondering if it wasn't *too* conservative. Maybe she should wear the lingerie after all.

The phone rang again.

"Hey," Pope said. "Y'all miss me yet?"

"What do you mean?"

"Henry didn't tell you?"

"Tell me what?"

"I moved to New York. I've already got a place down there."

"Where are you now?"

"Well, I'm in Edson, packing up the rest of my shit," he said. "Listen, what time are you coming up to the Millhouse tonight?"

"I'm not."

"But your skis are still up there, remember?"

"Yeah, I know," she said, wincing. "I guess I'll pick them up next week."

"But I'm gonna see you tonight, right? Hey, it's my last night in town."

"No," she said, "I can't. I've got other plans. Sorry. But good luck in New York." She was proud of the distance in her voice.

"Are y'all mad at me or something?"

"No. Why?"

"I don't know. You just sound different, that's all. So what are you doing that's so important?"

"I've got dinner plans."

"What, with your family again?"

"No."

"Oh," Pope said after a pause. "Look, can y'all do me a little favor tonight?"

"I don't know. What is it?"

"Well," he said, laughing sheepishly, "I kind of already moved my bed down to New York. Can I stay with you tonight?"

"Oh, Pope, I won't be here tonight. I'm staying at my folks' house. You know, with the mill closing and all, they're moving up to Newport tomorrow, and I've got to help them pack up first thing in the morning."

"Caroline, I really wanted to see you."

"And I'd like to see you, Pope. I'm sorry, but I'm sure you'll find someplace to stay. I've really got to go now. Bye." She hung up before he could respond. Lighting another cigarette, she took the plastic bag of lingerie out of her drawer.

HENRY CALLED McManus at home to thank him for the pictures.

"Oh, yeah," McManus said. "Didn't you get a kick out of the ones with John when he was seasick?"

"They were great. An amazing shade of gray."

"Hey, I heard that what's-her-face, Tyler Beckett, mentioned you on the Letterman show. I didn't see it myself—we're asleep by then—but a lot of folks mentioned it the last couple days."

"Yeah?"

"No, I'm lying," McManus said. "So what's this about you writing songs with her?"

"Actually, she played an old one we wrote years ago. I did start playing a little guitar again, though."

"It's about time."

"Well, I don't know what I'm going to do with it or how long it'll go on," Henry said. "Look, I wanted to ask you a favor. Could you start sending me up copies of the Austin *Chronicle*? I'd like to get an idea of what's going on."

"Sure. Any chance of your coming here?"

"Maybe. Everything's kind of up in the air right now."

"But at least you're playing guitar again," McManus said.

"Yeah, as of yesterday. So I don't know where any of this is going. It's all bullshit, anyway. You're the lawyer —you should know that."

"Not everything, Henry. Just most things."

"Whatever."

"I'll have my secretary take care of the *Chronicle* business tomorrow."

"Thanks."

"And remember, Henry, you're welcome to stay with us as long as you like."

"Thanks," Henry said. "Now I've got to run. Believe it or not, I've got a date with a twenty-one-year-old."

"Nice-looking?"

"In fact," Henry said, "she's really good-looking."

"Well, good for you. Enjoy yourself for once."

SHE WAS TURNING slowly in front of her mirror, making sure the outline of her garter belt didn't show, when Rachel pushed through the door and caught her smoking.

"You agreed to no smoking when you moved in here."

"I only smoke in my room," Caroline said. "I don't smoke in the rest of the apartment."

"It'll make everything stink!"

"I've been smoking for months and you haven't noticed. Besides, you let somebody smoke in here last night. I could smell it."

Rachel smiled. "That was Henry."

"What?"

"I invited Henry over for a few drinks yesterday afternoon. Naturally, I let him smoke. He was here for quite a while." She smiled again. "So where are you two going tonight?" she asked sweetly.

"I don't believe you!"

"You can ask Henry, though I'm sure he'll deny it."

Caroline marched out of the apartment and pounded on Henry's door.

He opened it, still wet from the shower, with a towel wrapped around him. "Hi. I think you're a little early," he said, smiling.

"Did you sleep with Rachel yesterday?"

He laughed. "Why? Did she say I did?"

Suddenly Caroline was both relieved and embarrassed. "Oh, Henry, I'm sorry. I had no right to say that."

"No problem," he said. "Uh, look, I'm freezing. I've got to get ready. See you in a bit, okay?"

"Okay."

"By the way, you look great."

She smiled at him and shut the door. Back in her apartment, Rachel was waiting for her. "Well?"

"He just laughed," Caroline said, then walked into her room and locked the door.

HENRY HAD one clean, pressed shirt in his drawer— his funeral shirt, he called it, ready for infrequent jacket-and-tie affairs. He'd bought it when he first moved back to Edson and had never worn it. He picked the pins out, pulled the cardboard from under the collar, and unfolded it. He thought it was a good thing he'd seen Caroline beforehand, because otherwise he would've worn dungarees and a flannel shirt. He had a clean pair of khakis and his brand-new pair of Tanner work boots.

As he finished dressing, he wondered what it was that had seemed different about Caroline a few minutes earlier. Maybe he'd just never seen her in high heels. He couldn't pinpoint it, but something was different.

His fingers burned as he buttoned his shirt. He combed

his hair, then peeked out through the window shade and saw sleet coming down in the lamplight. He still had ten minutes to himself, so he poured a shot of bourbon and sat down to work on Tyler's piece a little more. The hot water from the shower had softened his fingertips, and he split a blister on a treble string. He put on the last Band-Aid in his shaving kit, then went down the hall.

WHEN HENRY KNOCKED on Caroline's door, he smelled of shampoo, cigarettes, and a little bourbon, and she liked it. They decided to take her car because of the weather.

"I've got to stop for cigarettes," she said. "Do you need anything?"

"No, I'm all set."

As Caroline drove to Martello's, the sleet fell heavily and clung to the wipers in clumps. She parked in front, and Henry offered to run in and get the cigarettes. One side of her wanted to walk in and buy them herself, no matter who saw her do it, and the other side wanted to stay dry. "Thanks, Henry," she said. "That would be nice."

After he returned and they started for the restaurant, the sleet let up a bit. The Civic's heater was blowing nois-ily, and Caroline pushed in the cassette that was already in the player—Henry's first album.

He quickly turned it off. "You don't mind, do you? It

makes me uncomfortable to listen to myself. I only listen to my stuff when I have to. For me it's like work, and tonight I just want to have some fun. Is that okay?"

"Of course. I'm sorry. I didn't know."

"Well, there's no way you could know. Don't worry about it. It's just a weird thing I have."

Now she nervously wondered what she'd do wrong next, and they drove without speaking for a couple of miles. "Are you hungry?" Henry finally said.

"I sure am."

"I haven't been to this place in years. They used to have great lamb chops."

"Oh, I love them too!" she said. "I had them there last month with Pope." And that stopped the conversation until they reached the inn.

The restaurant was in an old farmhouse, and the main dining room occupied what had been the living room. Caroline and Henry were led to a table near the hearth, where a powerful fire burned and fat logs snapped like cap guns. Henry ordered bourbon on the rocks, Caroline a vodka tonic.

"You look different tonight," he told her, "but I can't put my finger on it."

"Different? How?"

"I don't know. That's just it. Did you do something with your hair or makeup or something?"

"I don't think so," she said.

"I'll figure it out. Whatever it is, you should keep doing it. I mean, I'm not telling you how to look. It's just that you look great. Well, you always look great, but there's just something different tonight." Henry felt awkward blurting this out, and he realized he was as nervous as he used to feel before an important show.

Caroline looked down toward her drink. When Henry lit a cigarette from a book of matches, she noticed the Band-Aid and reached for his hand. Turning it palm up in the candlelight, she saw the pale white blisters and knew he'd been playing guitar again. "Oh, Henry," she said softly.

He shrugged when he saw she understood. "They're still pretty tender. It takes a while to build up good calluses."

Caroline was happy to think the strings she'd bought might've helped get him playing. "Do you think you'll start performing again?"

"I don't know." He shifted uncomfortably in his seat, as he'd done when they listened to his third album together. "Tyler wants me to write songs with her, and I've been thinking about it. That's all. I could stand to make some money, though."

"God, that's wonderful!"

"Yeah, well, I don't know if I can do it anymore." He took a deep drag and held the smoke in a long time. He seemed to be weighing the possibilities. "Who knows?"

She lit a cigarette, certain that nobody from Edson was in the restaurant. "I'm sure you can, Henry. That's really exciting!"

"I don't know." He sipped his drink and looked around the room. The light was low, coming mostly from the fire. Short white candles inside clear glass globes were placed on every table, and in theirs he could see the distorted reflection of both Caroline and the fire. This was the first time he'd been out to a real dinner in months, and he liked the pressed white tablecloth and cloth napkin, the glint of candle flame in the polished silverware, and the warmth of the fire on the side of his face.

They both chose the lamb chops, and Henry ordered another drink for himself and a bottle of wine for the two of them. He told her about the photographs McManus had sent, and talked a bit about his last trip to Alaska. "Unfortunately," he said, "the season was kind of aborted."

"What do you mean?" she asked.

"We had an accident with another boat, and that was it for fishing."

"My God! What happened? Were you hurt?"

"Nah, just banged around. Nobody really got hurt. It was night, and the fog was heavy." He ground out his cigarette and lit another. "You almost couldn't see the bow from the stern, so we weren't rushing things, just trying to make some headway logging lights and following charts. It was right after midnight, and I'd just gotten off my watch and gone below to get some sleep, so I didn't actually see what happened. But evidently the running lights of the other seiner appeared out of nowhere in the fog, heading straight for us, nose to nose, bow to bow, no time to change course, and we collided head-on. All I remember is the impact knocking everybody out of their bunks and freezing water pouring into the forecastle, bodies on top of bodies in this absolute darkness. I'd never been so scared in my life, and you wouldn't believe how cold that water is."

"Oh, my God!" she said. He ran his hands through

his hair, pulling it back in his fingers, and she noticed the beginning of a widow's peak. It made her think of the differences between them, not just in age but in experience. Suddenly she felt like a silly waitress from Edson who'd never done anything and probably never would.

"Well," he said, "it sounds more dramatic than it was. The worst thing was that it was early August, just when the fish were really starting to run. I could've made a hell of a lot more money."

"And that's when you came back to Edson?"

"I couldn't think of anywhere else to go."

The waitress brought salad, and they put out their cigarettes. While they were eating, Henry told her the story of running out of gas in the skiff with McManus.

"Where's he now?" she asked.

"McManus? He lives in Austin. He's a lawyer."

"Have you ever been there—to Texas?"

"Sure, a lot when I was touring," he said. "How about you?"

"No. I've been to Boston once or twice, but that's about it. I've never been anywhere."

"I like Texas, especially Austin. I think you'd like it. It's different than here. Ever had deep-fried alligator tail?"

"Alligator? You're kidding me."

"No. It's really good. It's more of a Louisiana thing, but you can get them in Austin."

"Could I see those pictures from Alaska sometime?" she asked. "I can't imagine you with a beard."

"Well, it was kind of sparse. You've got to look pretty hard to see it."

The firelight flickered around his face, and she could see the thin shadows of crow's-feet, tiny black threads, when he turned his head at a certain angle. After a couple glasses of wine, Caroline relaxed and didn't worry about what she said. They both laughed easily, and before she knew it, they'd finished their espressos and were ready to leave.

As they crossed the icy parking lot to her car, he took her hand so she wouldn't slip.

"Jesus," he said, "it's gotten colder, hasn't it?"

"I know." She hoped he might kiss her before they got into the car, but he didn't. Though the sleet had stopped, the roads were still slick and she crept along, not even chancing third gear.

She turned the radio on low, and Henry hummed along with the tune. She couldn't recall seeing him so at ease.

"Hey, you want to see those Alaska photos tonight?" he suggested.

"I'd love to."

"Who's doing this song?" Henry asked. "I've heard it before, by somebody else."

"I don't know. I've never heard it before."

"Yeah; somebody had a minor hit with this years ago."

Metallic-blue police strobe lights scraped the sky as they approached the Edson town line.

"Looks like an accident," Caroline said, slowing the Civic even more.

"No, I don't think so," Henry said, sitting up. "It's a roadblock. I can't believe it. On a night like this, in this weather? This is really bush league."

A cruiser was parked on each side of the road, stopping traffic in and out of town, and a few cars were lined up behind each one. The drivers stood outside, waiting to be tested for drunk driving.

"Are you okay?" Henry asked Caroline.

"I think so. You had most of the wine."

"I know I'm a little over the line, but you're the one behind the wheel."

"Oh, look who we get—Junior Dells."

"Didn't you go to high school with him or something?" Henry asked.

"He was a year behind me. Oh, Henry, I don't like this. What if I don't pass the Breathalyzer?" She ground out her cigarette.

"Look, first off, don't say anything. Just answer his questions and do what he tells you, but that's all. Don't try to act friendly. Man, this really pisses me off. I'll bet cars are off the road all over the fucking map, and these yahoos come up with this shit instead of helping people out of ditches."

Wearing a clear plastic poncho over his uniform and a clear plastic cover over his campaign hat, Junior Dells dismissed the car in front of them, then motioned Caroline forward with his flashlight.

When she was alongside him, Caroline rolled down the window.

"License and registration, please."

Caroline handed him her license and dug the registration out of her glove compartment. Henry saw that her hands were trembling, and he suddenly felt furious.

"Have you been drinking tonight, ma'am?"

"I had a glass of wine with dinner, Junior," she said.

"Please step out of the car, ma'am." He handed back her license.

Caroline wasn't sure what made Henry snap, but he was out of the car before she was.

"What is this bullshit, *Junior?*" Henry said, loud enough for everybody to hear. He crossed his arms on the icy roof and leaned his chin on top of them. "It's nearly ten o'clock. Does your mother know you're out this late?"

Some of the waiting drivers, people who'd known Junior all his life, covered their mouths and snickered. Caroline was too horrified to do anything but stand beside the car and wrap her arms around herself. All she could think of was the trouble Henry was getting into.

"Let's see some identification, my friend," Junior Dells said, walking around the car to Henry. Henry turned to face him. He took a deep drag and blew the smoke out slowly. Junior Dells held the flashlight right in his face. "Just who the hell do you think you are?" he demanded.

"Me?" Henry took another drag, then bowed and said, "I'm just an old musician talking to some fat young asshole on a cold fucking night."

The drivers waiting to be tested started laughing, and Junior spun around to glare at them.

"I've already got two smart-mouth drunks in the cruiser," he said to Henry. "One more word outta you and you're gonna join them. Now—show me some ID!"

"My ass," Henry said softly.

"What did you say?"

"My ass, Junior," he said again, looking away.

"What are you saying?" Junior shouted.

"I think you ought to kiss my ass."

Junior Dells brought his flashlight down across Henry's forehead. Henry felt his knees buckle, but then threw a short right that pushed Junior's nose up toward his eyes and dropped him. They were outside the beams of headlights, and few people saw it clearly.

In tandem, the two cruisers' radios scratched out an emergency call about a four-car collision on Edson Hook Road, and the senior officer hollered from the other side of the road. "We've got a Code Three, Junior. Let's move—now! Where *are* you?"

Junior hauled himself to his feet, holding his bleeding nose. Henry could've popped him with a left, but he'd heard the police business come over the radio and he knew he had to stay clear. Junior brushed himself off, then grabbed Henry by the coat and slammed him against the side of Caroline's car. Henry felt jerked around like a marionette. He hadn't expected Junior to be so strong.

"I'll fix you later," Junior said. Then he gingerly padded over the ice to the cruiser, trying not to slip in front of the people he'd stopped.

"Maybe," Henry muttered, "but I don't think so."

The two cruisers sped off, throwing up a thin spray of rock salt, sand, and ice.

Caroline stood quivering on the other side of the car, staring at Henry. Her instinct told her to rush to him, but she couldn't move. She sensed that Henry now felt the same immunity her brother Stephen must have felt—that there could be no consequences for his actions in Edson anymore, because he was leaving and wasn't coming back. Maybe he didn't even know it himself.

People had walked back to their cars and were pulling out past Henry and Caroline. She climbed into the Civic, found a cigarette, and tried to keep her hands from shaking so she could light it. Henry got in, rubbing the knuckles of his right hand, and slammed the door shut. "Let's go," he said.

"Yeah," Caroline said as she put the car in gear. "You're bleeding."

"Yeah?" He touched his forehead. "I can kind of locate the area." He turned on the overhead light and pulled his visor down to check himself in the mirror.

"Are you okay?"

"It's not too bad." He flipped the visor back up, cracked the window, and lit a cigarette.

"Junior was about to take you down to jail."

"Yeah, I know."

"Then what would you have done?"

"I don't know," he said.

"I mean it!" she said angrily. "What would you have done?"

"No idea. I hadn't thought that far ahead. I just knew it wasn't going to come to that. I don't know why."

"Henry, let's just go back to the hotel and watch a movie or something. I can put something on your forehead. Rachel's going to be out most of the night."

"Okay, that sounds good."

It was as if he had been lifted out of town, she thought.

He wasn't drunk, not really. He was just no longer part of Edson, and she wanted to be with him wherever he drifted. She drove north up Main Street and took an early turn across from Thurman's Meats to avoid a steep hill, then parked in her spot in the back of the hotel. They walked through the empty lobby and up the stairs, holding hands, not talking. On the second-floor landing he suddenly stopped, turned her toward him, and kissed her for a long time.

"LET'S GO to my place," he said outside her door. "You never know when Rachel's going to show up."

"Okay," she said. "Do you want some popcorn or something? I could microwave it and bring it over."

"Do you want popcorn?" He unlocked his door and they walked in.

"No, not really."

"Do you feel like a drink?" He turned on the bathroom light to check his forehead in the mirror. The bleeding had stopped. He wiped the dried blood off with wet toilet paper and walked back out.

"Yes," she said. "I'm still a little shaky. How about something I've never had before?"

"I'm afraid I don't have the greatest variety to choose from. How about a bourbon and ginger—ever had one of those?"

"That sounds good. I want to get drunk tonight." Taking her coat off and sitting down on the bed, she lit a cigarette. He mixed her drink and handed it to her. "Henry, when are you leaving?"

He stopped pouring his bourbon. "I don't even know if I am. How'd you know I was thinking about it?"

"I just knew."

"Well, to be honest, if I write with Tyler, I'll have to move down to Danbury for a while. But I think that would be just for a couple weeks."

Caroline sipped her drink. That didn't sound horrible, and at least he'd be coming back. "Are you going to?"

"Yeah, I think so," he said, as if he'd finally solved a problem.

"She doesn't live in Danbury, does she?"

"No, she lives in New York, but I don't go there anymore. It's just this thing I have. Danbury was her compromise, though it's not exactly halfway between here and New York."

He sat down on the bed, and Caroline moved closer to him and put her hand on his shoulder. "What happens after Danbury?"

"I don't know. Maybe I'll head down to Austin."

"To visit or move?"

"I'm not sure. Move, I guess. I wanted to stay here, but with the mill gone, it won't be long before it starts looking like a ghost town. It doesn't even know it's dead. I mean, it's not going to dry up and blow away like you see in westerns, but it'll be run by a skeleton crew. Like the dairy farms scraping by up north these days."

"My family already found a place in Newport, and they're moving up tomorrow. My dad and older brother got jobs at the mill."

"And you're staying here?"

"I'm not going with them, that's for sure. On top of everything else, my little brother left home the other day and we still don't know where he is, and I'm really starting to get worried. But I've been up there for family things—it's where my cousins live—and I don't like it much. I'd rather be on the coast."

"So what'll you do?"

"I don't know. Stay at the Pilot Inn for now." She took a big drink of her bourbon and ginger, then set the glass down on the floor and ground out her cigarette. Thinking of everyone moving away all at once—Henry, her whole family—Caroline had to fight back tears. She held his face with both hands and kissed him, pulling him back onto the bed with her. He wrapped his arm around her. They kissed again. "Make love to me, Henry."

"I don't know if I can love anybody anymore."

She got up on her knees to unbutton her blouse. "You don't have to love me, just *make* love to me." She tossed her blouse on a chair and fell on top of him. She held his head in her arms and kissed him fiercely, her dark hair falling over his face.

THEY LAY together for a long time without speaking. She listened to him breathe, a soft rumble deep inside his chest. The room had never seemed so sad before.

"Henry, I meant what I said. I do love you."

"I wish I could say I love you, Caroline. It's not that I don't want to. It's like I just don't have all the parts or emotional equipment or something."

"Henry," she said, "take me to Austin with you."

"What?"

She took a drag of her cigarette. "I mean it. When you go to Austin, take me with you. We can get a place together."

"What? Don't joke around like that, please."

"I'm not joking," she said. "I've got some money saved up, and I could get a job waitressing, so you wouldn't have to do anything but write. I'm a good cook, and you said you feel great when we're together, that you can relax. And you liked the way we made love, didn't you?"

Henry got up from the bed. "I loved the way we made love. Do you want a drink?"

"Yes, please. You know, you don't have to be in love with me for us to live together. I just want to be with you, to do what I can for you. You at least *like* me, right?"

"Caroline, I care about you a lot. I just don't think it would be very fair to do something like that." He picked up their glasses and went to make fresh drinks.

She had been surprised at how soft his skin had felt, and how smooth, like a baby's. Now, watching his naked body as he stood there in the kitchen, she saw how frail his skinny frame looked. The muscles from fishing were still there, but they were small and tight and looked like they had nothing to cling to. "I don't care about fair," she said. "No relationship's a perfect fifty-fifty split, is it?"

"I think you're crazy," he said, laughing, and handed her the drink. "But let's not talk about it anymore. I'm not even sure I'm going to Austin." He climbed back into bed and kissed her.

HENRY WOKE to the smell of coffee. Caroline stood by the stove, wearing only his white button-down shirt. He coughed, and she turned to face him.

"Morning," she said happily. "Ready for some coffee?"

"Sure. What are you doing up?"

"I don't know. I just woke up, wide awake, about an hour ago. I watched you sleep for a while, then I got up." She brought a mug of coffee to him and sat down on the bed beside him. She rubbed her hand across his stomach.

"You know," she said, "you were crazy last night."

"What do you mean?"

"With Junior Dells. He's going to be looking for you now."

Henry shrugged. "Well, he'll have to look down in Connecticut."

"What got into you, anyway?"

"I'm not really sure. It was just that for the first time

in my life I knew everything was going to be all right, that I could do just about anything I wanted." He laughed. "I have no idea where *that* came from."

"And you still feel that way?"

"Yeah, I think so. I just don't want to think about it too much."

"What are you doing today?" she asked.

"Well, I've got to call Tyler and tell her I'll do it, then I've got to go to the bank, then I've got to work on the guitar. How about you?"

"I'm off work, but I'm helping my parents get packed up."

"Want to do something about supper?"

"I could cook us something," she offered.

"No, let's go out," he said, thinking he didn't want to see Rachel.

"Okay."

He finished his coffee and slipped his shirt from her shoulders. He lifted the covers and she climbed in.

It was late morning by the time she left. Henry poured another mug and called Tyler.

"My fingers are killing me," he said when Lizzie put her on.

"Hey, that's the best news I've heard all morning," she said.

"I've got a bridge for that one verse in E," he announced. "And I've got some other ideas."

"Good boy. So when are we getting together?"

"How's tomorrow?" he said.

"Perfect. How long can you stay?"

"As long as you need me," he said.

"Henry, that makes me so glad. Man, I've been going crazy. The panic's really on, but I knew you'd come through for me. I can't tell you how much this means. So thanks, really."

"Yeah, well, I'll see you tomorrow. What time are you getting there?"

"I don't know," she said. "Early afternoon."

"Good. See you then. . . . Hey," he said before she hung up.

"What?"

"No guarantees."

"I'm not worried," she said. "I can't wait to see you."

He picked up his guitar. The blisters had gone down a little in the night, but they still felt like tiny burns. He started to play, but it was too awkward with the Band-Aid, so he ripped it off and tried to avoid using that finger. He played the piece in E he'd worked on the day before. But when he came to his bridge, he had to jump to a different chord to spare his finger, and a completely new melody came to him. He played it a few times and decided it suited Tyler's style better than the first one. He figured he'd keep the original for himself and build a song around it. The new bridge had a slightly more accessible feel to it, a little more pop, and Tyler would love it. Henry laughed to himself and set his guitar down. There was no point now in not depositing the check.

In the hotel lobby, he gave Crazy Betty all the cigarettes he had. She stared at the two packs in disbelief.

Downtown was filled again with ex–mill hands standing around in groups, sullen and silent. He stopped at Martello's for cigarettes, then continued on to the bank. Despite the depressing atmosphere, Henry felt full of energy, and even the cold didn't bother him.

Kancamagus Savings was the only bank in town. It was run entirely by women, and Henry recognized most of them from when he'd started playing at the Millhouse years before. Smiling, he waited in line with the check and a deposit slip in his shirt pocket, and finally he stepped up to the window. "You think this bank's still gonna be around next week?"

The teller looked up sternly. "I should hope so." She was tall, with a face as round as a pie, and her tight little eyes peered down at him.

"All right," he said, sliding the check and the deposit slip to the teller. "I'll take a chance on you, then."

"Do you have any identification?"

"Identification?" Henry said. "It's a *deposit*—a cashier's check. And I've been banking here off and on for years. You know who I am."

"Then you know we require positive identification for every transaction."

"You do understand I'm trying to put five thousand dollars *into* your bank?"

"But you want to take out two hundred in cash, sir."

"Which is already covered by my savings account."

"Well, no matter what you say, it's still our policy to see positive identification."

"Of course it is," Henry said, smiling, "and rightly so.

You can't be too careful these days." He took his driver's license from his wallet and slid it across the counter.

CAROLINE CHANGED into dungarees and a sweatshirt and work boots, then lit a cigarette and sat down to relive every moment of their lovemaking. Henry's scent was still on her, and she could taste him. When she finished her cigarette, she put on her parka and walked over to her parents' house. Much of the furniture was sitting in the yard or on the sidewalk, where her father was loading a U-Haul truck.

"Are you all packed up?" he asked.

"No."

"Then what are you doing here? I told you to pack up your things before you came over."

"I'm here to help you pack."

"We can manage just fine, thank you. You'll only slow us down if you're not ready when we're done."

"But I'm not going."

Her father sat down in the wing chair, now on the curb, that Father Heire always used when he visited. "How many times do I have to tell you?"

"Daddy, I'm not moving."

Her mother came out the front door with a taped-up box from the liquor store. It said *Kitchen* on the side in red Magic Marker.

"Mom, have you heard from Stephen?"

"No, dear." She put the box down in the back of the truck, then looked at her husband. Caroline could tell she was on the verge of tears.

"Marjorie, we don't have time to jabber," he said. "Harold and I start work in the morning, so let's finish loading up. Caroline isn't coming with us. Go get the rest of those boxes from the kitchen."

He stood up and climbed into the truck, where he wrapped the television set with a blanket. Her mother had gone, leaving Caroline alone on the sidewalk, and she walked into the street behind the U-Haul. "Dad?" she said.

He jumped down and walked past her into the house without a word.

"Dad!" she called after him.

"YOU SHOULD'VE seen Pope last night," Larry said, sitting in the office at the gas station.

"How's that?" Henry said. He'd been telling Larry about his plans with Tyler and his night with Caroline and the run-in with Junior Dells.

"Oh, you know—a couple days away, and he's already a New Yorker. More important," Larry said, waving his hand in front of his face as if he were shooing a fly.

"That's just Pope." Henry looked out the window and

saw Junior Dells drive up to the pumps in his Ford Explorer. "Uh-oh. It's the sheriff."

Larry motioned for Henry to stay inside, but he got up and followed him.

Junior Dells saw Henry and got out of his car. He was dressed in street clothes. "Hey, I know you."

"No you don't," Henry said.

Larry set the pump on automatic and walked quickly back into the office.

Junior Dells grabbed Henry by the jacket and threw him against the car. The back of Henry's head snapped back and thunked against the window. "Okay, smart-ass. Ain't no car accident gonna help you now."

"Beg to differ," Larry said from the other side of the car. He was holding the station's baseball bat in a perfect Carl Yastrzemski batting stance, his arms extended and high, his shoulder almost choking him under his chin. "This would qualify as a car accident, and it sure looks like this windshield's coming in high and outside."

"Don't!" Junior said, letting Henry go. "Hey, I've got a job interview in Portsmouth in forty minutes. I can't drive down there with a shattered windshield."

"No shit. Apologize to Henry, Junior," Larry ordered, the bat still cocked, "or it'll be a drafty ride."

"Okay," Junior said. "I'm sorry."

"Henry," Larry said, "take what he owes and shut off the pump. Junior, you pay up and clear out." He walked around to the driver's side. "And this never happened, right?"

"Right."

"Good luck with your interview."

Junior didn't say anything, just got in his car and drove off.

"Nice batting," Henry said. "I'd better get a move on. I've got to do my laundry and get packed."

"You're staying at the Hilton, right? Isn't that what you said?" Larry leaned the bat against one of the pumps.

"Yeah."

"So let them do your laundry for you."

"Yeah, for an arm and a leg."

"For Christsake, Henry. You're writing songs with Tyler Beckett. Go in style for once in your life."

"Well, maybe you're right." He thought of what McManus had said about enjoying himself, then tried to think of a decent restaurant that would be open on Monday. Caroline would know. Or maybe they should stay in and cook the partridge before he left.

CAROLINE WALKED back to the hotel, trying to decide if she'd rejected her parents or they'd rejected her. She climbed the stairs to her apartment, relieved that she didn't have to work that night. She just wanted to see Henry again.

In the living room, Rachel was sitting on the divan as if she'd been waiting for her. "I want you to move out," she said.

"What?" Caroline said, stunned. "Why?"

"You lied to me when you moved in here. You told me you didn't smoke."

Caroline suddenly felt weak. She sat down across the room from Rachel and unzipped her parka. "I didn't smoke when I moved in." She paused. "But this is about Henry, isn't it?"

"What are you talking about? This is about lying about smoking. It stinks in here! I can't stand it!"

"Okay, I'm sorry," Caroline said. "Really. I promise I won't smoke in the apartment."

"Too late."

"What do you mean?"

"It's too late," Rachel said. "Donna Collabretta's moving in at the end of the month."

"Henry turned you down and made love to me," Caroline said. "That's why you're doing this."

"Oh, don't be ridiculous," Rachel said. "Do you really think I couldn't steal Henry from you in, like, five seconds?"

Caroline didn't think so, but she wasn't sure. She stood up and walked into her bedroom, pulled the door closed, and lit a cigarette. After all, it didn't matter now. The lease was in Rachel's name.

"Remember," Rachel called from the living room. "I want you out of here by the end of the month."

HENRY'S CAR looked like an igloo after a sleet storm. Nearly an inch of clear, bumpy ice covered the body, and he couldn't even open the doors. He took out his Swiss Army knife and started chipping the ice away from the door handle on the driver's side and along the seams. When he yanked the door open, some of the ice cracked and fell onto the seat, which he brushed clear before getting in. The clutch was sluggish, and he needed both hands to move the gearshift into neutral. He pushed down on the gas pedal, lifted his foot off, and turned the ignition. The engine shuddered slowly at first, then caught as Henry worked the accelerator up and down. Once the car was idling smoothly, he turned the blowers up to high, lit a cigarette, and switched on the radio. Soon after the heat came on, the window ice began to melt, falling away from the warm glass in sheets, and Henry got out to scrape off the whole car. That much, at least, was ready for tomorrow.

SHE HEARD the footsteps in the hall and knew it was Henry. Running out into the hall as he was opening his door, she threw her arms around him. He led her inside and shut the door behind him.

"Hey," he said. Her head was buried in his shoulder, but he pried her away and saw she was crying. "Hey, what is it? What's the matter?"

She burst into sobs and couldn't talk. He led her to the bed, sat down beside her, and took her hands in his. "Caroline?"

"R-R-Rachel," she managed, but then couldn't continue.

He pulled her close. "Take your time."

Her shoulders shook and she hiccuped, then she quieted and placed her hands on her lap. "Rachel wants me to move out."

"You have a fight?"

"I don't know. She says it's because I've been smoking in my room."

"It sounds like she's your mother. Besides, she let me smoke over there on Saturday."

"I know, but that was different. She was trying to seduce you."

"How do you know that?"

"I'm not stupid." Caroline took out her cigarettes.

"Well, you can smoke as much as you like in here. You want a drink too?"

"Why not?" she said, lighting up. "God, I have to be out by the end of the month. I have no idea where to go."

"Oh, that's no big deal," Henry said, getting up to fix the drinks. "You can stay here."

Her eyes widened, and she jumped up from the bed and threw her arms around him. "Oh, Henry! Do you mean it?"

"Sure," he said.

"It'll be cozy. I can do all the cooking and cleaning and stuff, and you can just concentrate on your writing."

"You don't understand, Caroline. I'm going to Danbury tomorrow, remember? I won't be here."

"Oh, that's right." She took the glass he held out to

her and looked down. "I can't believe you're leaving already. Then what?"

"Probably Austin," he said. "But I'm not sure." He took a spare key off a hook in the kitchen wall and gave it to her. "I do like the idea of you staying here, Caroline."

"You know, I wouldn't get in the way—in Austin, I mean."

"I know." He took her drink and set it on the counter, then pulled her close and kissed her.

SHE REACHED across the blanket for his pack of Kool Milds. "I don't know what you see in these menthols. It's like smoking a breath mint."

"You get used to them."

The afternoon light was fading. Henry switched on the lamp, and that made it seem even darker outside.

"What kind of songs are you and Tyler going to write? I can't see her singing about mill towns."

He laughed. "Not all my songs are about mill towns. In fact, there isn't even one on that third album. I must be slipping."

She lit her cigarette. "So what'll you write about?"

"I don't know. I'll just do what I've always done—dredge up something miserable from my past, change it around a little, and call it a song." He laughed again. "Sounds grim, doesn't it? I could do a lot of divorce songs about the ol' ex. There's bound to be plenty of rhymes for 'lying sack of shit,' don't you think?"

"Henry, that's awful."

"Yeah, yeah, I know," he said.

"Don't you ever write about the future?"

"What do you mean?"

"You know, daydream about things that might happen and write about that. I'm always doing that, thinking about stuff in the future. But it's like you're always looking backwards." She paused. "Could I get another drink?"

"Yeah, sure," he said, throwing the covers off and taking her glass to the counter. Writing about the future was something he'd never thought about. Maybe because she was so young, she had only one direction in which to look—ahead. It seemed strange to think that he had two. Even when he was just starting out, he wrote out of his own past experience, or someone else's. He handed her the drink. "Where can we go for supper?"

"Let's go shopping, and I'll cook you something here."

"Really?"

"Sure. I love to cook," she said. "Let me just finish this drink."

"There's no hurry. I've still got those partridge in the fridge. How's that sound?" He climbed back under the blankets and lay back, staring at the ceiling.

"I'd like that," she said. "I haven't had partridge in years."

As he lay there imagining the evening ahead of him —Caroline cooking dinner while he played guitar—it seemed impossible that so much time had passed, that he wasn't twenty-two years old and getting ready down at the Millhouse later that night. And for all he knew, except for picking up his things after he finished writing with Tyler, this would be the last night he spent in Edson.

He thought about the drive in the morning and just what he'd take, and what he'd take to Austin after that. Austin would be mild through the winter, and after spending most of the summer in the frigid Ketchikan rain, he'd had enough of the cold. He pictured himself in January in a little ground-floor apartment off Guadalupe at sunset, sipping a Shiner Bock, playing guitar on his patio, nothing but a sweater on.

WHEN THEY WOKE, the room was cold and they made love in the gray morning light. Neither said a word. Later, when he got up to make coffee, he told her to stay in bed, then pulled on his bathrobe and turned up the space heater. He looked out the window and smiled when he saw it was snowing. The drive would be longer, but it would be prettier. He lit a cigarette, coughed, then took two cups from the cupboard and set them on the counter.

"Can I do anything?" she asked, brushing the hair away from her face.

He shook his head, then the phone rang and he picked up the receiver.

"You're still coming, aren't you?" Tyler said. "You're not going to chicken out on me, are you?"

"Why would I chicken out?" he said. "I should get down there around two."

"Yeah, well, have you checked out the weather?"

"What, the snow? It looks like it just started."

"Didn't you see the weather report last night?"

"I don't have a television."

"We've got five inches down here already, and two storms are headed for New York. It could be blizzard time, Henry."

"I'm from New Hampshire, remember? I *know* how to drive in the fucking snow," he said. "I'll be there around two, maybe three." The water started to boil.

"Well, you're all set at the Hilton. Lizzie took care of everything. And don't forget your swimming trunks."

"See you later," Henry said, and hung up. He didn't have any swimming trunks. He poured the water into the large filter, and while it sifted into the pot he turned the radio to a classical station. "Did you hear anything about a snowstorm coming?"

"No. Why?"

"Tyler says New York already has five inches. There's supposed to be two big ones coming. It's snowing out there now."

"I haven't heard anything about it." She looked up at him. "What time are you leaving?"

"Around ten," he said, handing her the first cup of coffee. "That was a good wine last night, wasn't it? Good call."

"Thanks," she said. "It's what my mother buys when we have Father Heire over for dinner."

He poured a cup of coffee for himself and climbed back in bed with her, still wearing his bathrobe. "You know," he said, "I've never cowritten a song that I'd put on one of my records. I mean, not like they're bad songs or anything. I like that one Tyler sang on Letterman."

"Me too."

"But I wouldn't record it, though I'm glad she's going to. I don't know why I feel that way."

"Are you worried about cowriting?" she asked.

"A little, but I think I know what she needs. I'm really more interested in what happens after that."

"Do you think you'll really go to Austin?"

"I wish I knew. I keep going back and forth. Mostly I want to start writing my own songs again, though I don't know what I'll do with them. Does any of this make sense to you? I'm just thinking out loud."

"It makes sense to me."

"Well, that makes one of us." He put out his cigarette and lit another.

THEY WERE taking a steamy shower together when the tears came. Caroline tried to hide it by accusing him of getting soap in her eyes, but they both knew she was crying.

They took turns toweling each other off, then Henry dressed and threw some other clothes into his travel bag.

Caroline put on the clothes she had worn the day before. "I can forward your mail down to Danbury," she said.

"I'll call you with the address. I don't know how long I'll be there, but you should send the bills and everything. That'd be great."

"I'd be glad to," Caroline said. "It's time to leave, isn't it?"

"Yeah."

"Okay, let me dry my hair and I'll walk you down to your car."

"Sure," Henry said. He finished packing while she was in the bathroom. When he looked up, she was standing in the doorway, looking at him.

"I left my coat over in my apartment."

"Here," he said, going to his closet. "This'll work." He handed her his blaze-orange hunting coat and helped her slip it on. He zipped it up for her and said, "Are you going to stay here tonight?"

"I thought I would, given Rachel and everything."

"You should. Just push my stuff off to a corner or something and make yourself at home. Larry can help you move your stuff over, if you've got anything heavy. I'm glad you're staying here." Henry slid his arms into his leather jacket and picked up his travel bag and his guitar. "You all set?"

Caroline shook her head, then said, "Yes."

She was crying by the time they got to the bottom of

the steps, and she followed Henry across the parking lot to his car, already blanketed with several inches of new snow.

Henry stowed his bag and his guitar, then closed the trunk and pulled her close to him. "I'll call you when I check in," he whispered.

"I love you, Henry," she said. "Be careful."

He kissed her, and as she pulled away from him the snowflakes gathered on her cheeks and eyelashes.

CAROLINE SAT at a window in Henry's apartment for a long time, watching the snow pile up on the rooftops and roads and cars. Snowplows lumbered up and down the narrow avenues, their yellow flashers twirling. After a while she made herself a cup of tea. She took it back to the bed, undressed, and climbed back under the covers on Henry's side.

THE SNOW came down heavily, and the roads got bad once Henry crossed the New Hampshire line into Massachusetts. The interstate hadn't been plowed, and traffic was forced into one lane for miles at a stretch. He turned off in Sturbridge to stop at the discount liquor store, and what normally would've taken ten or fifteen minutes became an hour's delay. He pushed on steadily through the afternoon, driving right into the oncoming storm.

By three in the afternoon, the winds had kicked up and snow was blowing across the road like a veil. Henry was exhausted. Creeping along the interstate, he had to drop from third gear into second, and when he got to Bristol, Connecticut, he decided he'd gone far enough. He took the Queen Street exit and pulled into a Motel 6 at the end of the ramp, right behind a Denny's. Eight inches of snow covered the lot, and the desk clerk switched on the NO VACANCY sign after handing Henry his key. Carrying his gear up to the room, he called the Hilton to tell Tyler he couldn't make it all the way, but she hadn't checked in yet, so he called her office.

"It's a total mess down here too," Lizzie said. "Tyler won't even leave until tomorrow morning, maybe the next day. It's a blizzard out there, Henry."

"Yeah, I know," he said. "I've been driving in it all day."

After hanging up, he slipped into his old motel routine. He turned on the television without the sound, then dug his shaving kit out of his bag. He set it on the bathroom shelf and took out the things he'd need that night, lining them up on the sink. He put his jacket back on and went outside to fill up the ice bucket. When he returned, he washed the road grease off his face, then removed his boots and lit a cigarette. The room was still freezing, so he turned the thermostat as high as it would go and poured himself a big drink.

Starting to feel hungry, he stretched out on the bed, then reached over and dialed his number in Edson.

"Where are you?" Caroline said.

"How'd you know it was me?"

"I just knew. Are you okay?"

"Yeah, I'm all right." He looked around the room, at his guitar case on the floor, his travel bag on the table. "But I'm not going to make it to Danbury today."

"I know," Caroline said. "Where are you?"

"At a Motel 6 in Bristol. Just like old times—crappy motels in weird places."

"After you left," she said, "I looked up how far it was to Danbury, and I had the feeling you wouldn't make it that far. They still don't know how to take care of snow south of New Hampshire."

He could hear the space heater blazing away on the other end. "How's everything at the apartment?"

"Fine. I haven't seen Rachel all day. I only went over there once, and she was out someplace."

"Caroline," Henry said, his voice trailing off. He looked around at things not meant to last longer than a night or two—thin white towels, styrofoam cups, tiny bars of soap, a single book of matches—and remembered all those nights he'd spent on the road.

"Yes?" she said after a few moments.

"Sorry," he said. "I just drifted off for a while there. It's been a long day." Something inside his chest started to ache, like an old injury resurfacing, but he couldn't tell exactly where it was. He kneaded his knuckles against his rib cage, trying to zero in on the spot. "Have you started moving your things in?"

"Of course," she said, giggling. "The minute you left."

"Yeah?" He realized he'd never seen her room and didn't even know what her things were like.

"Sure. I'll get Larry to help me with some stuff when he gets home."

"Great. Well, I think I'll finish this drink and go get something to eat. Can I call you later?"

"Of course," she said. "When?"

"I don't know. A couple hours? And let me give you the number here, just in case." He glanced down the dial of his phone and recited the numbers. "Room two twelve."

"I'll be here. If not, it just means I've gone down to Martello's for a minute or I'm moving something. Leave a message and I'll call you back."

"Okay. I'll talk to you soon." Replacing the receiver, he turned up the volume on the television and poured another drink, happy he'd stopped off in Sturbridge. The small room was already warm, and he felt cozy, almost as if he were home—though at least here he had a television. Then again, at home he didn't have to drink out of a styrofoam cup. Everything's a trade-off, he thought. He lit another cigarette and watched the Weather Channel for a while. They were predicting this could be the blizzard of the decade and showed storm footage taken earlier that afternoon in New York City.

At some point, worn out by the drive, he dozed off without expecting to. When he woke up, the room was stifling and, except for the television screen, dark. He pulled open the blinds and watched snow gusting in the lights of the parking lot. He picked up the phone again and dialed his number back in Edson. A couple hours had passed, and he wanted to hear her voice again. His machine clicked on, and he heard himself say, "This is Henry. Please leave a message and I'll get back to you as soon as I can." The voice sounded as thin and distant as a transistor radio.

There was a click, then Caroline picked up. "Henry?"

"Hi," he said. "I fell asleep."

"I'll bet you needed it," she said. "Hey, you won't recognize your apartment. Larry and I are redecorating." She laughed. "We decided it needed a feminine touch."

"What did you do—tie ribbons around my guns?"

"Oh, you'll see."

He could hear Larry laughing in the background. "Well, whatever. Knock yourself out." He held the phone receiver snug under his chin and poured another bourbon. "You heard the latest weather?"

"Just that more snow's coming. The Pilot Inn didn't even open today, so I didn't have to worry about that."

"Well, I was just watching the Weather Channel, and they're talking two major storms tonight, one from the southeast and one from the east, and it's blowing like crazy down here. They're saying this could be worse than the blizzard of '78. The tides are up and the moon is full. Are you okay?"

"I'm fine. We're used to it, right? But it sounds like you could be there for a couple days. Will you be all right?"

"Yeah, everything's cool," he said. "There's a Denny's

next door and a convenience store right down the road. The motel's got cable, and I've got plenty of cigarettes and sour mash. The situation's under control."

"Know what else I did this afternoon?" She sounded excited. "I bought a pack of Marlboro Lights at Martello's."

He laughed. "And did the world stop?"

"No, stupid," she said. "But I sure thought it was going to."

"Have you heard anything from your brother?"

"Not yet, but I'm not as worried as I was. Stephen's smart, and I just know he'll be okay."

They talked a while longer. Henry made her promise to call before going to sleep, then he put on his coat and walked over to Denny's.

ON HIS WAY BACK after eating, the wind was blowing so hard it nearly toppled him. The motel parking lot was completely full, the snow drifting around the cars lined up snugly side by side, and Henry remembered a photograph he'd once seen of a herd of cattle feeding in a blizzard on the plains.

Back in his room, he hung up his coat and dusted the snow off. The vague pain in his chest, he suddenly noticed, had disappeared. He poured a drink, then took his guitar out of its case and pulled a chair over to the window, where cold air was seeping in through the casing. Turning off all the lights, so he could see outside as the storm blew on, he sat down with his guitar and started playing, the snow swirling in little dust devils on the walkway outside his door.

Every so often, he stopped playing to sip his drink and then curve his sore fingertips over the rim of the styrofoam cup, pushing them down into the tiny ice cubes for some relief. He sat there in his dark room, watching the snow come down, playing until he had to rest his fingers, and thought about the days ahead. He would call Caroline before he went to sleep that night, and he would talk to her many times before the roads cleared and he could leave for Danbury, as the blisters faded and the calluses started to form.

A NOTE ABOUT THE AUTHOR

Bill Morrissey has recorded several albums for Philo/Rounder Records. He lives in Boston with his wife, Ellen. This is his first novel.

A NOTE ON THE TYPE

This book was set in Fournier, a typeface named for Pierre Simon Fournier, a celebrated type designer in eighteenth-century France. Fournier's type is considered transitional in that it drew its inspiration from the old style yet was ingeniously innovational, providing for an elegant yet legible appearance. For some time after his death in 1768, Fournier was remembered primarily as the author of a famous manual of typography and as a pioneer of the point system. However, in 1925 his reputation was enhanced when the Monotype Corporation of London revived Fournier's roman and italic.

Composed by PennSet,
Bloomsburg, Pennsylvania

Printed and bound by The Haddon Craftsmen,
Scranton, Pennsylvania

Typography and binding design by
Dorothy Schmiderer Baker